THE CURSE
OF THE
ICE SERPENT

JON MAYHEW

BLOOMSBURY

LONDON NEW DELHI NEW YORK SYDNEY

For Brian Buckley, Andy Gardner and Steve Stapleton –
'All for one, and a packet of Scampi Fries, probably'

Bloomsbury Publishing, London, New Delhi, New York and Sydney

First published in Great Britain in January 2015 by Bloomsbury Publishing Plc
50 Bedford Square, London WC1B 3DP

www.bloomsbury.com
www.JonMayhewBooks.com

Bloomsbury is a registered trademark of Bloomsbury Publishing Plc

A CIP catalogue record for this book is available from the British Library

ISBN 978 1 4088 5423 5

Typeset by Hewer Text UK Ltd, Edinburgh
Printed and bound in Great Britain by CPI Group (UK) Ltd, Croydon CR0 4YY

1 3 5 7 9 10 8 6 4 2

CLAUDIA

Then I shut down my computer, because
I didn't want to spend all night constantly
reloading the MeVid page to see how many
views I'd gotten.

But I couldn't help myself. So after
half an hour of pacing back and forth in my
room and reminding myself to stay totally
down-to-earth no matter how huge I got, I
went back online...

WANT TO LEARN ALL ABOUT THE SHOCKING DISCOVERY
I MADE WHEN I WENT BACK ONLINE?
Check out my next book, THE TAPPER TWINS GO VIRAL!!!!
COMING SOON!!!! (And it's MY BEST BOOK EVER!!!)
xxoo Claudia

ABOUT THE AUTHOR

Geoff Rodkey is the author of the *New York Times* bestseller *The Tapper Twins Go to War (With Each Other)* and *The Tapper Twins Tear Up New York*, as well as the acclaimed adventure-comedy trilogy The Chronicles of Egg. He wrote the screenplays for the hit films *Daddy Day Care*, *RV*, and the Disney Channel's *Good Luck Charlie, It's Christmas*, and has also written for the educational video game *Where in the World Is Carmen Sandiego?*, the non-educational MTV series *Beavis and Butt-Head*, Comedy Central's *Politically Incorrect*, and at least two magazines that no longer exist.

Geoff currently lives in New York City with his wife and three sons, none of whom bear any resemblance whatsoever to the characters in *The Tapper Twins*.

'The names of those bold sailors thronged into his memory, and it seemed to him that beneath the frozen arches of the ice he could see the pale ghosts of those who never returned.'

Jules Verne, *The Adventures of Captain Hatteras*

CORNWALL,
1815

CHAPTER ONE
FIRE IN THE SKIES

'It's a flying machine,' Dakkar said, his voice low with wonder. 'It has to be!'

A distant, shadowy ball floated towards him and wings fanned the air on either side of the shape but, even from his vantage point at the top of the castle, Dakkar found it hard to pick out any detail. A faint crackling, like the spitting of fat on a hot frying pan, drifted from the shape.

'Gunfire too!' Dakkar murmured. He crouched beside the castle wall. It was called 'the castle' but Dakkar's home was more like a fortified tower on the top of a cliff. Below him, seagulls wheeled and screamed over the waves that lashed against the rocks. '*Two* flying machines!'

Little puffs of black smoke erupted from one of the outlines in the sky. Two red-and-yellow-striped balloons floated closer. Dakkar could see baskets dangling below the balloons now. The 'wings' were made of material stretched between wooden poles that flapped back and forth, propelling the balloons towards the castle. The balloon nearest him appeared unarmed – or at least made no attempt to fire back. He snatched up a telescope that lay at his feet and peered through it with a gasp.

The attacker bore a black flag emblazoned with a letter C, encircled by a snake, a trident poking up behind it.

'Cryptos!' Dakkar hissed under his breath. 'I should've known!'

Cryptos! The evil organisation run by Count Oginski's brothers. They were hell-bent on ruling the world. Count Oginski, Dakkar's mentor, had been part of the group once but had turned his back on them, sickened by their increasingly terrible deeds.

Now Dakkar could make out a figure huddled low in the basket of the nearest balloon. Bullets buzzed close to the wickerwork, sending fragments spinning off. The marksmen in the other craft were finding their range and would soon pepper the basket with lead.

Dakkar sprinted across the flat roof of the tower and into the doorway that led down to the top floor of the building. There by the door stood a rack of rifles – he grabbed one, plus some powder and shot. He hurried back to the roof, trying to pour powder down the rifle barrel as he ran.

By the time he reached the battlements, the balloons were overhead, drifting round the castle towards the sea. Dakkar fired at the Cryptos balloon, piercing it at the top. He grinned as the material ripped, letting hot air out through the rent.

The Cryptos Guard leaned out of their basket, trying to locate the culprit. Strong-looking men with fierce faces. Dakkar ducked behind the wall to reload. He popped out again and took a shot at the ropes holding the basket to the balloon. His bullet flew wide but clipped one of the men in the shoulder. A guard turned his rifle on Dakkar, the bullet pinging off the stonework close to Dakkar's cheek.

Another shot rang out and Dakkar saw one of the Cryptos guards clutch his hand.

Dakkar grinned. *Georgia must have heard the shots and grabbed a rifle*, he thought. Georgia was Dakkar's only friend apart from Oginski. She was the niece of Robert Fulton, the famous American inventor, and had saved Dakkar's skin on two adventures now. The gun smoke from the ground suggested that she'd taken cover in one of the outhouses that nestled at the foot of the castle.

The Cryptos balloon swung and jerked on its ropes, sending it veering into the castle walls with a crunch. It floated away again and, as it did so, a rifle barrel poked out of the basket and a final shot cracked into the other balloon. The Cryptos balloon drifted further away and Dakkar sent a warning shot across its path. Georgia followed suit.

'They're getting away!' Dakkar yelled down to Georgia, but horror replaced his excitement as he saw a flicker of flame lick up the fabric of the other balloon. This balloon began to fall, gradually crumpling in on itself.

Dropping his rifle, Dakkar hurried into the building and down the stairs. Leaping steps two and three at a time, he threw himself into the hall and outside.

The balloon lay on the open, grassy cliff top in a blaze of flames. Some distance away, the basket lay on its side. A figure scrambled out, dragging several heavy bags and sacks.

Georgia gripped her rifle, her red hair glowing in the light of the fire. She wore a simple cotton gown but didn't seem to notice the chill wind blowing off the sea.

'Good shootin', Dax,' she said, giving him a wink. She nodded at the man staggering towards them. 'Looks like we got company.'

Dakkar felt his cheeks redden. 'I wish you wouldn't call me that,' he muttered.

Georgia raised her rifle. 'That's far enough, mister,' she said. 'Now suppose you tell us who you are and I'll decide whether or not to shoot you as a trespasser.'

Dakkar frowned at the portly man. Quite elderly, short and well fed, he looked the most unlikely aeronaut. His dark, curly hair and thin, waxed moustache suggested a city gentleman, used to comfort and fine living.

The man gave a short bow. 'Forgive me, my dear,' he began. 'I did not mean to drop in on you so unexpectedly.'

'Well, you did. So who are you?' Georgia said, not softening her tone.

'My name is Borys,' said the man, giving another bow. 'May I thank you for saving my life!'

'You can thank me,' Georgia said, her rifle poised. 'Then you can tell us what you were up to in that balloon.'

'The last time we saw a contraption like that,' Dakkar said, stepping forward, 'it carried a villain with poorer manners!'

'Prince Dakkar,' Borys said, bowing again with a flourish of his hand that made Dakkar feel he was being mocked. 'It's such an honour to meet you!'

'How do you know who I am?' Dakkar said, the blood draining from his face.

'He knows you because he knows me,' said a voice from behind Dakkar.

He turned and saw Count Oginski filling the doorway of the castle. The big man looked stern. He leaned on his walking stick and glared at the visitor.

'Who is he, Oginski?' Dakkar said, glancing from his mentor to the man.

'He didn't give you his full name,' Oginski said, narrowing his eyes. 'Dakkar, Georgia, meet Borys Oginski, another of my wicked brothers.'

CHAPTER TWO

RUMOURS FROM THE NORTH

Borys Oginski didn't look as though he'd leapt from a burning hot-air balloon only a few hours ago. With growing confusion, Dakkar watched this portly, self-satisfied gentleman who was now sitting in Oginski's lounge dressed as if he were attending a state ball. Wearing a rich woollen jacket and contrasting silk scarf wrapped around his thick neck, his hair was slicked with oil and his moustache waxed to sharp points. Unlike the tall, brooding Oginski, Borys was plump and jovial. His eyes twinkled and he looked as if he were laughing at some untold joke that only he knew.

How can he be related to Count Oginski? Dakkar wondered.

Borys poked his finger through the bars of the cage that stood near the fire. 'This is a strange pet,' he said. The creature inside resembled a small featherless bird with leathery wings for arms and a long face split by a grinning mouth full of needle-sharp teeth.

'It's called Gweek,' Dakkar said, reddening. 'It doesn't like the cold so we keep it in here. I acquired it on my last ... expedition ...'

'It comes from the world below this one,' Borys said, whipping his finger away from the snapping little beast. 'The world that was ruled by our brother Stefan.'

Dakkar swallowed and stared hard at Gweek, who squawked and worried at the bars of the cage. Although Dakkar had been responsible for Stefan Oginski's downfall, the ruler of the underworld was a cruel tyrant set on conquering the surface world with his monsters. Dakkar had been right to stop him but now Borys's stare made him feel guilty.

'You have a cosy hideaway here, Franciszek,' Borys said, breaking the awkward silence.

Oginski's face hardened. 'Don't get too comfortable. You aren't stopping long.'

'Franciszek, Franciszek, my brother,' Borys said, shaking his head and making his curly, black hair wobble. 'Is that the warmest welcome you can find in your heart?'

Yes, why is Oginski so set against this brother? Dakkar wondered. How could this man be a threat? He was a stark contrast to the other two brothers Dakkar had met. Borys seemed soft, more concerned with comfort than anything else.

'Yes – given that the last time we met in Paris you tried to poison me,' Oginski growled. 'You'll forgive me if I'm a little guarded this time.'

Poison? Dakkar had never heard this story. He knew

that the Brothers Oginski had become villains of the worst kind after the Russians had invaded their land, killed their parents and burned their castle and estates. He'd heard the story of how they all vied for the affection of the beautiful Celina, leaving their beloved land on a quest in her name. They returned to find smouldering ruins and Celina gone. From that day on, they became pirates, mercenaries, killers and thieves, using their talents and knowledge to hit back at Russia wherever they could. This life hardened them and they began to lust for power themselves. And so the organisation known as Cryptos was formed, each brother calling himself Count Cryptos and all seven of them plotting to conquer the ruling nations of the world.

'Ah, Paris,' Borys said with a sad smile. 'How glad I am now that we weren't successful. I regret my old ways, Frank. I want to put the past behind us.'

'A likely story.' Oginski snorted, pouring himself a glass of port from the bottle Borys had helped himself to a moment earlier. 'You and Tomasz would sell our grand-mother to keep yourselves in the lap of luxury.'

'Who is Tomasz?' Dakkar cut in before the conversation left him far behind.

'Another brother.' Oginski nodded at Borys. 'His identical twin. They were always at each other's throats and yet united against the rest of the world. Believe me, Dakkar, these two are more deadly than the rest of the Oginski clan put together. And more dishonest.'

Borys gripped the arms of his chair and angry red spots

flamed in his cheeks. 'So only *you* are capable of changing? Only *you* can be redeemed?' he spat. 'The great Franciszek Oginski can become a saint but his brothers remain devils?'

'Are you saying you've abandoned the Cryptos mission?' Oginski sneered.

'Did you not see the Cryptos balloon chasing me?' Borys said, half rising in his seat. 'They would have killed me but for these youngsters here!'

'The last two Oginski brothers we've met weren't so eager to make friends,' Georgia said, her arms folded. She had been silent up to now, watching Borys's every move.

'And those brothers – *our* brothers – have ended up dead at your hands,' Borys said, waving an accusing finger at Dakkar, Georgia and Oginski. 'Aren't you tired of the bloodshed? Can't all this end?'

'We didn't seek them out,' Dakkar said crossly. 'It was they who tried to kill us. If they'd left us alone … If they'd lived in peace …'

Borys slapped the arm of his chair. 'Exactly!' he said. 'That is all I want to do but it seems some of us have other ideas.' He looked hard at Oginski, who lowered his gaze to his drink.

'Maybe you do.' Oginski sounded unimpressed. 'Who was trying to shoot you down?'

'Tomasz's guards.' Borys's voice was barely a whisper.

Dakkar looked at to his mentor. 'So what's new?' he said. 'Didn't Oginski just say that you hate each other?'

'Yes, but this time it's different. Tomasz has become even more power-crazed,' Borys said. 'He's planning something terrible. I managed to stall his plan and fled but he chased me.'

'What is he planning?' Dakkar asked. His mouth felt dry as he spoke.

'He's going to harness the Heart of Vulcan,' Borys replied, looking pale now.

'And what in the world is that?' Georgia said, narrowing her eyes.

'A Thermolith,' Borys said, jumping up and striding over to the fire. 'I believe you have possession of the Eye of Neptune, a Voltalith, a fragment of rock from the stars that crackles with electrical energy?'

Dakkar swallowed hard. It was true that they had such a thing. Dakkar had been forced to retrieve it from the ocean bed by another Oginski brother only last year. The Voltalith was used to power the *Nautilus*. Dakkar tried not to give anything away but Borys stared at him as he spoke, a slight smile playing round his lips.

'We know everything, boy,' Borys said. 'You think the Brothers Oginski don't communicate with each other?'

'The Heart of Vulcan is a similar rock fragment but it generates huge amounts of heat and never cools,' Oginski cut in. 'I'd heard tell of it but thought it just a myth until now.'

'The Heart of Vulcan exists all right,' Borys said, the wine glass shaking in his hand. 'A seething, glowing ball of energy!'

'Think how many hot-air balloons you could power with just a fragment of it,' Georgia whispered.

'Or how many steam engines without the need for tons of coal,' Dakkar added. 'If you broke it up, it could drive a fleet of steam ships …'

'We had the Heart of Vulcan in our grasp,' Borys continued, a glint in his eye. 'But what Tomasz was planning filled me with dread. I am sick of slaughter and destruction.'

'Was Tomasz going to use it to power a weapon?' Dakkar said.

'He has already built a huge fortress that can fly using many hot-air balloons.' Borys shook his head. 'Imagine being able to sail above each major city of the world – you could drop bombs, rain fire and destruction down on them without anyone being able to fight back. Cities would be reduced to rubble, their populations brought to their knees. Tomasz would become invincible, unstoppable. Put simply, he would rule the world from the skies.'

'That's awful,' Georgia gasped. 'Nobody could touch him. Armies and navies would be powerless.'

'I had to stop him,' Borys said, tears glistening in his eyes.

'What did you do?' Oginski said, watching Borys closely.

'He needed the Thermolith to power his creation,' Borys said. 'I took it and hid it in an ice cave in Greenland then fled for my life. But Tomasz will be searching for it, believe me.'

'That's why the Cryptos Guard weren't shooting

directly at you,' Georgia said slowly. 'Tomasz wants you alive.'

'Tomasz never was the smartest of the two of you,' Oginski snorted. 'You always had the brains, Borys. Tomasz couldn't find his own shoelaces without your help.'

Borys's cheeks coloured red and he glared at Oginski. 'Tomasz is still our brother,' he said. 'To underestimate him would be a grave mistake.'

'He's right. Sooner or later Tomasz will work out where the Heart of Vulcan is,' Dakkar said in a low voice.

'If we can get the Heart of Vulcan before he does,' Borys said, pouncing on Dakkar's eagerness, 'then think of the chaos and suffering we can avoid.'

'We've *got* to find it before he does!' Dakkar said, looking towards Oginski.

The big man held up his hand. 'You are impetuous, my boy,' Oginski said. 'We don't know how close Tomasz is to finding the Thermolith.' Oginski gave Borys an icy stare.

'We don't even know if he *is* looking for it.'

Borys shook his head. 'Ever the stubborn mule, Frank,' he said. 'You think I arranged for Tomasz's men to shoot at me? You think I set fire to my own balloon, right on the edge of a cliff, so that you'd believe me? You think I'd try such a stupid gamble, just to win your confidence?'

Oginski stared back at them, twirling the glass in his fingers.

'One thing you *do* know about me, Frank, is that I'm not stupid,' Borys said, glaring at his brother. 'I don't do stupid things. I don't take risks.'

'Nevertheless, we are not going charging off to Greenland on some fool's errand because Tomasz *might* be looking for trouble,' Oginski said, putting his drink down. 'I need time to think.' He stalked out of the room and slammed the door behind him, making Gweek squawk.

Borys turned to Dakkar and Georgia. 'I fear we don't have the luxury of time.'

CHAPTER THREE
A DECISION

The heavy wooden workbench that ran the length of one wall in Dakkar's workshop creaked as Georgia settled herself on to it. Oginski had given Dakkar this room to practise building all kinds of mechanical marvels and Dakkar treated it as a haven too. Cogs and springs littered the work surfaces and plans jostled for space on the walls. Strange white hieroglyphs covered the chalkboard that stood in the corner next to a couple of ragged armchairs.

'Do you think we can trust him?' Georgia said, twirling a spring between her fingers. 'What he said was right. If Oginski can change his ways, so can Borys. And why shouldn't he want to?'

'I don't know,' Dakkar replied, leaning heavily on the bench. 'Oginski seems adamant. He's spent the last two nights guarding Borys's room. He wouldn't do that unless he had good reason. He looks terrible.'

'He's still recovering from his encounter with

Napoléon's guards,' Georgia said, nodding. Oginski had
received near fatal wounds when they fled from Elba,
pursued by the Emperor Napoléon's toughest soldiers.

'What if we sent word to Cutter?' Dakkar said, lifting
his head. 'They could come and keep an eye on Borys.'

Cutter and his men were Cryptos Red Faction, elite
guards who fought with Oginski before he turned away
from the organisation. Each member of the Red Faction
owed Oginski his life and had sworn to serve him. Since
Oginski had reformed, they had kept their distance, living
in a cove along the coast and hoping he would return to
the fold. But Cutter's men were loyal to Cryptos too and
this made any involvement with them complicated.

'I don't think we need to keep an eye on Borys,'
Georgia said, throwing the spring back on to the bench.
'We need to persuade Oginski to find this Thermolith
before Tomasz does!'

A slight cough made Dakkar and Georgia turn. Borys
stood at the door, peering in. Dakkar looked over his
shoulder, expecting Oginski to be shadowing him.

'Your mentor is asleep on his chair outside my room,'
he said, as if reading Dakkar's mind. 'It seemed a shame to
wake him. Can I come in?'

Dakkar looked at Georgia and then nodded. 'He'll be
furious when he finds you've sneaked out of the room,'
Dakkar said. 'What do you want?'

'Ingenious,' Borys said, stepping into the workshop and
picking up a clockwork model of a dog. 'You are a clever
young man.'

'I have a good teacher,' Dakkar said, reaching out and grabbing the toy. 'Please be careful. It's ... delicate.'

'Explosive, more like.' Borys chuckled. 'How far does it walk before it goes off?'

'A few feet,' Dakkar muttered. He could feel his face reddening. 'It gives off a loud bang, a flash of light and releases a thick cloud of smoke. To cover a retreat.'

'It seems a waste to put so much effort into making something that does so little damage.' Borys gave a sly smile and gently took the toy back, squinting at it. 'But you work on ... bigger projects with my brother too?'

'Maybe.' Dakkar shrugged.

'You seem mighty interested in Oginski's inventions,' Georgia said, folding her arms.

'Tomasz will find the Heart of Vulcan, my dear,' Borys said, his face suddenly serious. 'He will find it and he will use it to conquer the world. If we're going to get it before him, we'll need all of Dakkar's ingenuity – and yours, of course. Oh, yes, Georgia Fulton, I'm fully aware of your famous uncle, Robert Fulton, and his part in the invention of the submarine called the *Nautilus*.'

'Robert Fulton's *Nautilus* was a mere toy,' Dakkar said. 'He tried selling it to Napoléon years ago but it didn't impress the emperor.'

'Don't play games with me. I'm not talking about the prototype,' Borys said, throwing up his arms in mock despair. 'I'm talking about the craft he perfected with Oginski. The one that works. The one that my brother Kazmer made them build before he died.'

Georgia and Dakkar stood in silence but couldn't help glancing at one another.

'If we're going to get to Greenland then the *Nautilus* is our best chance,' Borys said, his voice low. 'But she will need some modification – the waters there are cold and icy. I only want to help.'

'Even if we did want to help you,' Dakkar said, 'I won't go against Oginski. He's like a father to me. It's him you have to persuade.'

Borys shook his head. 'Tomasz must be stopped,' he said. 'If Oginski doesn't see this, we're all doomed.'

'So this is how you repay my hospitality, Borys?' Oginski said, his large frame filling the doorway. 'You sneak off while I'm asleep and try to turn Dakkar and Georgia against me.'

'I was merely trying to persuade them that doing nothing is madness,' Borys growled back. 'And they are totally devoted to you.' He gave a slight smile.

'I would trust either of them with my life,' Oginski said, his stern features softening.

'He does have a point, Oginski,' Dakkar said. 'The Heart of Vulcan is out there and Tomasz won't rest until he's found it. We *must* retrieve it before he does.'

Oginski raised a hand. 'Enough,' he said. 'Borys, I'd be obliged if you returned to your room. I need to talk to Dakkar and Georgia.'

Borys inclined his head. 'As you wish, my brother,' he said and sauntered out through the door, making Oginski step back for him.

'Oginski, believe me, we wouldn't have gone against you –' Dakkar began.

'We must find this Thermolith though,' Georgia cut in.

Oginski held up his hand again. 'Calm yourselves,' he said. 'I've thought long and hard and I can see that you're right. We can't ignore this. And as much as I have my reservations about my brother, I agree that we must give him the benefit of the doubt.'

'Yes!' Dakkar hissed, clenching his fists. He hated to admit it but the prospect of another adventure sent a thrill of excitement up his spine. Georgia beamed over at him too.

'But we must prepare properly,' Oginski said, labouring each word to press home the message to Dakkar. 'We can't just go waltzing off to Greenland in the *Nautilus*. Adjustments must be made to her.'

Dakkar's heart thumped in his chest. 'Borys said that he would help. We can get any modifications done in no time if we start now.'

'Ah, the enthusiasm of youth,' Oginski muttered, shaking his head and smiling. Dakkar thought he looked older at that moment, his hair greyer and the lines on his face somehow deeper.

'Are you all right, Oginski?' Dakkar asked, frowning anxiously at his mentor.

'Of course!' he replied, straightening his back and clapping his hands together. 'Now, call that reprobate brother of mine to my study. We must plan!'

'And, if you remember,' Georgia said, raising one eyebrow, 'get him to give you that explosive dog back …'

CHAPTER FOUR
LURKER IN THE DEPTHS

The secret sea cave that lay deep within the cliffs beneath the castle echoed with Borys's delighted laughter.

'I'd heard about this incredible craft,' he said, as he clambered aboard the *Nautilus*, 'but the rumours and descriptions from our spies didn't do her justice!'

'We tried to keep her as secret as possible,' Oginski muttered, throwing an almost comic look of alarm at Dakkar.

We were spied on by Borys and Tomasz and I didn't even notice? Dakkar thought.

'A truly amazing invention, Frank.' Borys ran his palm along the polished, watertight boards of the submarine. 'Such craftsmanship too.' He looked over to Dakkar and Georgia. 'I bet these two had more than a hand in her construction.'

Dakkar felt his cheeks flush with pride in spite of himself. Even Oginski appeared flattered by his brother's praise.

'I consider Dakkar and Georgia my partners when it comes to developing the *Nautilus*,' he said, a smile playing around his lips. 'They're brilliant students and even more original thinkers.'

The *Nautilus* bobbed, straining at her mooring ropes like a spirited young whale, eager to take them all out to sea. The submersible was essentially a long wooden tube made of close-fitting burnished planks. A tower rose out of its middle, housing a hatch in its top. She looked like no other vessel on the seas.

'I'll need to know everything,' Borys said, climbing up the ladder on the side of the tower to get inside. 'Maybe you could take me out in her, to begin with.'

'That makes sense,' Oginski said, but Dakkar noticed that his smile had faded and the haggard lines of pain and worry had returned.

The exclamations and murmurs of delight continued inside the *Nautilus* as they climbed down into the tower.

'So this is where the captain sits,' Borys said, tapping the chair in front of the helm. He peered through the porthole at the view ahead of the submarine. 'This engages the engine?' He gripped the brass lever at the side of the seat.

'Yes,' Oginski said, sliding into the chair. He pointed to a brass handle. 'And that's the ballast control.'

Borys frowned for a second, rapping his knuckles against the inside of the craft. 'Ballast?'

'The hull has two skins and a gap between ...' Oginski began.

'The gap fills with water, making the submarine heavier,' Dakkar finished the sentence for him. 'So she can submerge.'

'And that's how she sinks,' Borys concluded, beaming. 'Wonderful!'

'And when we want to surface, we pump the water out,' Oginski said, clearly flattered again. 'Allow me to demonstrate. Georgia, could you release us from our moorings?'

Georgia scurried outside, untied the *Nautilus* and scrambled back inside, closing the top hatch behind her. They all crowded around Oginski in the control room at the base of the tower and watched the water rise around them.

Dakkar grinned as he noticed Borys grip the back of Oginski's seat with whitened knuckles. *Not so self-assured after all*, Dakkar thought.

'Here we go,' Oginski said, turning the ballast wheel.

They sank into the dim underwater light then Oginski pushed the lever to *Full Ahead* and began to turn the wheel.

'But how does one see down here?' Borys said, squinting into the gloom.

Oginski gave a tight smile and turned a wheel mounted in front of the power lever. Outside, eight glass orbs rose out of the deck at the bow and stern of the *Nautilus*. Each contained a fluorescent jellyfish that cast a bright glow around the craft.

'The jellyfish never dim,' he said. 'It was Dakkar's idea.'

Once more, Dakkar felt a surge of pride and gave a smile, staring down at his feet as his cheeks flushed.

'Such ingenuity,' Borys said, peering out at the bubbles that frothed around the porthole. 'Look!' he cried, letting go of the chair and pointing to a shoal of silver fish flitting past. 'Beautiful.'

Oginski spun the wheel again and headed towards a dark shadow that showed the entrance of a sea cave.

'Originally, we used a second chamber to exit the cave,' Oginski explained. 'But with this larger vessel it was necessary to open a wider tunnel into the sea.'

'That must have been dangerous,' Borys said, still staring out into the cloudy waters.

'It was a tricky job. We had to use the Sea Arrows to blast through the rock,' Dakkar said and then winced as Georgia jabbed him with her elbow.

'Sea Arrows?' Borys said, glancing over to Oginski. 'I assume they're some kind of explosive device you can fire underwater? Wonderful!'

They entered the mouth of the newly excavated tunnel, where pale blue fronds of seaweed danced with the ebb and flow of the sea. The weed emitted an eerie glow that illuminated the tunnel.

'We cultivated the seaweed,' Georgia said, pointing outside. 'Encouraged it to grow in the tunnel.'

The *Nautilus* gave a sudden jerk as if she'd been snagged by something. Borys stifled a panicky yelp as bars loomed out of the gloom before them.

'Don't worry, brother,' Oginski said, grinning at Borys's

discomfort. 'A hook on the *Nautilus*'s hull snags a chain that lifts the gate. When we come back in, it'll fall closed again.'

The barred gate began to rise as the *Nautilus* drew nearer. A loud clunk reverberated through the craft, telling them that the gate had clicked open.

'Amazing,' Borys stuttered, mopping his brow with a lacy handkerchief.

Suddenly the closeness of the passage vanished and they plunged out into the open water, the *Nautilus* rocking slightly with the new currents.

'Dakkar, if you could take the helm, Georgia and I will show my brother the engine room,' Oginski said, rising from his chair and giving Georgia's pistols the briefest glance.

Georgia nodded and gestured to the hatch at their feet that led down into the main body of the submarine.

Dakkar slid into the warm seat and gripped the wheel, listening to Borys's continued cries of wonder as they climbed down through the hatch. He grinned and stared out into the waters.

He watched shoals of fish flit by and laughed as he sent the *Nautilus* ploughing through them. A pod of dolphins swept past the window, looping over and under the craft, making Dakkar dizzy as he tried to keep track of them.

The dolphins scattered suddenly as if in panic. Dakkar's smile froze as a flash of silvery green blotted out the seascape. He glimpsed a round, staring eye and long teeth. Then they vanished into the thick jungle of swaying weeds on the seabed.

Dakkar pulled the thick bung out of the speaking tube on his left. This was another new development. Huge lengths of tubing with a cup at each end snaked from the captain's seat into each cabin. When you talked down them, a person at the other end of the tube could hear you. The heavy stoppers were there in case the room at one end became flooded and the water rushed up the tube.

'Oginski,' Dakkar called down the tube, 'can you hear me?'

There was a moment's pause and then a reply. 'What is it, Dakkar?'

'We're not alone down here,' he said.

'Not alone?' Oginski sounded puzzled. 'What do you mean?'

But Dakkar couldn't answer. A confusing tangle of muscled flesh, teeth and staring eyes exploded from the weed below, heading straight for the *Nautilus*.

CHAPTER FIVE
TRAPPED

Dakkar sent the *Nautilus* spiralling into a dive. He could hear the creature's tough hide scrape the planks of the craft.

'Dakkar, what's happening?' Oginski yelled from below, forgetting to use the speaking tube.

'Something big has taken a dislike to us!' Dakkar yelled back. 'Load some Sea Arrows!'

'We can't!' Oginski shouted. 'You know they're kept in the explosives vault back at the castle. I didn't expect to have to use them. Just head back to the cave!'

With a hiss of exasperation, Dakkar slammed the drive lever to *Full Ahead*. The sudden acceleration pushed him back in his seat. Glancing out of the window, he saw the creature clearly now. It looked like some kind of enormous eel, wriggling its way towards them. The *Nautilus* was big but this monster made her look like a toy. Dakkar dragged his gaze forward, focusing on the entrance of the sea cave and hoping he could outrun the massive eel.

The dark cave entrance and the gateway grew clearer as the *Nautilus* hurtled towards them. Dakkar gripped the wheel, aiming the craft at the centre of the narrow entrance. The eel swam closer, teeth glinting in the silvery light. Dakkar ignored it. If his aim faltered slightly, he would plant the *Nautilus* firmly against the rock of the cliff and that would be the end of them all.

The tunnel mouth loomed around them, gaping to swallow them up. Dakkar allowed himself a fleeting smile of triumph. It vanished as another shape flitted across his path. A small, human shape.

Instinctively Dakkar swung the wheel to avoid hitting whoever it was but something thumped against the hull. Turning the wheel in this confined space was not a good idea. Dakkar wrestled with the steering but the craft crashed heavily against the tunnel wall, bouncing from side to side as she careered onwards. Every bump and crack made him wince. He could hear the yells from below as Oginski, Georgia and Borys were thrown around the cabins. Luminous seaweed slapped at the portholes and whipped the hull as the walls of the tunnel flashed by.

A metallic clunk told Dakkar that the gate to the cave had slid back in place then, in a cloud of bubbles, the *Nautilus* burst from the tunnel into the sea cave. Dakkar dragged the lever to reverse, his stomach lurching as the craft slowed.

'I think we're safe,' he panted, as Borys peered cautiously into the control room from the hatch below.

'For now,' Borys replied, looking pale and shaken.

Within an hour, they all met in Oginski's study. Dakkar and Georgia sat warming themselves in front of a roaring hearth. Gweek, appreciative of the extra heat, fluttered around the room, landing every now and then on someone's head or shoulder. Borys had insisted on making everyone some hot spiced port and now he stood by the fire, cupping a warm glass in his hands.

'That was a close call,' he said and took a sip of his drink.

'It was an eel,' Dakkar said, nodding. 'A huge eel.'

'And it's still out there,' Borys said, his face stony. 'I hate to say it but this has all the hallmarks of Tomasz. Like all the Brothers Oginski, he takes delight in breeding the most monstrous beasts and using them for his own ends.'

'Not all of us enjoy making such monsters but, I agree, it has to be one of Tomasz's creations,' Oginski said, twirling his glass so that the firelight played on the ruby liquid inside. 'That creature … it was so huge. We have native species that grow to considerable size but never that big. It's unnatural.'

'I saw something else too,' Dakkar said, shivering in spite of the fire and blankets. 'A human figure. I think we hit it.'

'A Qualar?' Georgia said.

'It couldn't be,' Oginski murmured. 'The Qualar are our sworn allies.'

'The Qualar?' Borys looked puzzled.

'It seems you didn't find out everything about our dear brother Kazmer,' Oginski said with raised eyebrows. 'The Qualar are a race of undersea people. They look like humans but have scales and green skin. Kazmer conquered them and treated them like slaves. He relied on the Qualar to herd and direct his monsters.'

'But they rose up and overthrew him,' Dakkar added. 'Their king, the Shoal Lord of Qualarium, declared us friends of the Qualar. They would never work against us.'

'There's a similar race of mermen,' Borys said, taking a sip of port. 'The Inuit natives of Greenland call them Qalupalik. They're small and primitive – but vicious. They rely on their strength of numbers to overcome larger enemies. Tomasz has them under his control.'

'If they're out there,' Dakkar muttered, wandering over to the window and peering out into the gloomy twilight, 'the seas aren't safe.'

'Tomasz won't give up,' Borys said, narrowing his eyes. 'Not until he has captured me and found the Thermolith.'

'Then we should get the first punch in,' Georgia said. 'These mermen are another reason why we should go and get the Thermolith before Tomasz does.'

'I have a map showing where the Heart of Vulcan is hidden,' Borys said and hurried out of the study up to his room.

A few moments later, he returned with a rolled-up tube. Slapping it down on the table, he unfurled it. Dakkar wrinkled his nose at the musty, faintly rotten smell.

'It's drawn on deer hide,' Borys said with an apologetic smile. 'I had to improvise in my haste.' He traced his finger over the crudely drawn lines. 'This is the port of Guthaven. I suggest we sail there first. The cave is several days' march from the port.'

'We're going to have a battle to get through the seas if Tomasz has control of such monsters,' Oginski said.

'Then let us master another element,' Borys said, raising his glass as if proposing a toast. 'Let us conquer the skies!'

CHAPTER SIX

THE APPROACHING STORM

The following weeks became a dizzying whirl of activity. Oginski and Dakkar thought Borys had gone mad when he first showed them what he proposed.

'How can the *Nautilus* fly?' Oginski scoffed. 'She's a seagoing vessel and too heavy for the skies.'

'Such a closed mind, Frank,' Borys had replied. 'Didn't I fly here? Besides, I'm not suggesting we transform the *Nautilus* into an aircraft, merely that we increase her capability.'

Borys unrolled some plans that had lain hidden in the map tube.

Oginski's jaw fell slack as he looked at them. 'But ... but this is the *Nautilus*,' he stuttered. 'Where did you get such detailed plans?'

'They were salvaged from the ruins of Kazmer's volcanic base.' Borys grinned. 'You should have tidied up after yourselves. We picked this up off the ocean bed in a watertight tube.'

'And you adapted them to …'

'To turn the *Nautilus* into a flying machine!' Borys beamed then his face fell. 'I brought them here as a token of goodwill. I could have left them with Tomasz.'

'Then let's find what we need and get cracking,' Oginski said, clapping his hands.

After a hurried visit to the nearest town for tarpaulin, sailcloth, twine and all manner of strange equipment, Dakkar and Georgia found themselves stitching and gluing sections of oiled cloth for hours on end.

'I'm an engineer, not a seamstress,' Dakkar hissed, flexing his numbed fingers after one particularly hard session.

'I'm with you there,' Georgia muttered, sucking her pinpricked thumb. 'I'd rather be working on the *Nautilus* down in the caves with Oginski.'

'That worries me too,' Dakkar muttered. 'I'm still not sure about our friend Borys yet Oginski works so closely with him.'

'I know what you mean,' Georgia said, wincing as she pricked her finger. 'But if we're gonna stop Tomasz from getting the Heart of Vulcan and ruling the world, we have to go along with him.'

Soon Dakkar and Georgia were called to help move huge lengths of piping, to solder and cut, hammer and tighten nuts and bolts. Oginski appeared to have forgotten that only a few days ago he was standing guard outside Borys's room. Borys seemed happy for Oginski to lead the modifications to the *Nautilus* using his plans, waving any of Oginski's queries away.

'I'm not sure,' Borys said. 'Do you think it will work?'

'Yes, yes,' Oginski replied. 'I just thought I'd check.'

'You're the genius, Frank.' Borys would smile, handing the plans back.

Dakkar watched uneasily as Oginski became more and more fixated on the work.

'Blood is thicker than water, Dakkar,' Borys said one day as they sat stitching more lengths of silk and canvas. 'Franciszek knows in his heart that we are allies now.'

Dakkar said nothing but continued to tug at the seam he sewed.

'Frank trusts me,' Borys continued. 'Even if you don't.'

Mealtimes were hurried and Dakkar tried to talk to Oginski about Borys but he was always close by. Finally, when Dakkar did manage to take his mentor to one side, he was clearly distracted.

'There isn't time for this, Dakkar,' Oginski had said dismissively, frowning at him. 'Tomasz is coming. Time is of the essence. We must strike first!'

'If you're expecting Tomasz to attack us,' Dakkar said, 'can't we call on Cutter and his men?'

'If it comes to it, I will,' Oginski said with an impatient wave of his hand. 'But we must concentrate on modifying the *Nautilus* first.'

'I've never seen him so intense,' Georgia whispered as Oginski stalked back down to the cavern to help his brother. 'He's like a man possessed.'

Once they had finished the sewing and stitching, Dakkar and Georgia had to coat each sheet with a molten rubber solution. It was hot and smelly work. Dakkar often felt dizzy and nauseous and had to take regular fresh-air breaks.

'This is worse than the sewing,' he complained to Georgia.

Finally, they found themselves down in the *Nautilus* fitting a small furnace into the engine room. It reminded Dakkar of the black stove that glowed away in the kitchen. Pipes ran from the furnace and disappeared into the hollow hull of the craft. Outside, wooden pods housed the fabric they had spent so long stitching.

'The furnace is specially designed to superheat the air through those pipes,' Borys explained. 'To begin with, gas in the pods will fill the balloons that you've made. Then we shall use a mixture of hot air and gas. If our calculations are correct, the balloons should be able to lift the *Nautilus* high into the sky.'

'*If* your calculations are correct?' Dakkar said, frowning. 'What if it all blows up in our faces?'

Borys gave a shrug and a grimace. 'The furnace and the pipes will also heat the *Nautilus*,' he said, hurriedly distracting Dakkar from his doubts. 'We've insulated the sub's walls with a thin layer of duck down. The icy waters of the Arctic won't chill *us*!'

'But how will you stop the furnace from using up all the oxygen in the *Nautilus*?' Dakkar said, undeterred.

'You are a clever young man. The furnace is so efficient

that it uses very little oxygen,' Oginski said. 'In addition, this device helps!' He pointed to a box on top of the furnace. The box had windows cut into it that were covered in steel mesh. Dakkar could see a white powder inside.

'Saltpetre?' Dakkar said, recognising the powder.

'When heated, it absorbs the stale air that we breathe out and gives off fresh oxygen,' Borys said. 'With this, we can reuse the air we breathe.'

'But we'll still have to refresh our air supply from outside at regular intervals,' Georgia said, narrowing her eyes.

'Of course,' Borys murmured, looking a little crest-fallen. 'It's not perfect.'

'And what's this for?' Georgia asked, holding up a steel spike with a handle on one end.

'Fish or fowl,' Borys grinned, patting his ample belly. 'Anything we can slide on to it and cook over the flames of the furnace!'

'Enough of this,' Oginski said impatiently. 'Are we going to stand around debating the merits of this and that, or are we going to finish the work and get ready to test her?'

Later that night, Dakkar stood at the top of the castle, peering out to sea. Georgia stood next to him.

'I'm exhausted,' she said, leaning on the battlements that lined the edge of the roof. 'Oginski says that the modifications are done and we can test her tomorrow.'

'He seems so feverish, so eager to begin this quest,' Dakkar said. 'Yet he was the most sceptical when Borys first appeared. I don't understand why he's changed.'

'Maybe he's realised,' Georgia pointed out.

'Realised what?'

'That Tomasz isn't going to leave us alone while we're harbouring Borys,' Georgia said, pulling her coat closer about her. 'And that the sooner we find the Thermolith, the sooner we can be rid of both of them.'

'You could be right ...' Dakkar began. 'Shh! Listen!'

'What?' Georgia whispered. 'I can't hear anything.'

'There,' Dakkar hissed. Above the rumble of the waves against the cliffs and the buffeting of the wind there came a shrill screech like a seabird, but Dakkar could have sworn it sounded like words.

'You've got the hearing of a bloodhound,' Georgia smiled. 'And the common sense. There's nothing there. Maybe just gulls or something.'

'Maybe.' Dakkar shrugged. 'But I can't shake the feeling that we're being watched.'

'I know what you mean,' Georgia said, shivering a little.

'I don't see why Oginski doesn't just call for Cutter,' Dakkar said. He looked out into the darkness.

'From what you've said, Cutter's men aren't reliable,' Georgia replied. 'They'd protect Oginski but would let Tomasz take Borys if they had to.'

'I hate just sitting here, waiting,' Dakkar said, slapping his hand on the stone wall.

'You see? Oginski isn't the only one who's impatient,' Georgia said, turning to go downstairs. 'Come on – time to get some sleep.'

Dakkar followed her but another noise made him freeze on the spot. This time a whisper drifted up from the darkness. He ran back to the edge of the roof and stared over. All he could see were the black outlines of the outhouses and the distant horizon.

'I'm sure there's someone down there,' he muttered.

'Dakkar, what are you doing?' Georgia snapped as he barged past her and down the stairs.

'Come with me,' he hissed. 'And grab a rifle.'

The building was cloaked in darkness apart from the odd oil lamp sitting in a wall alcove and on the table in the main hall. Georgia and Dakkar snatched up a rifle each from the rack that stood at the bottom of the stairs and hurriedly loaded them.

'What did you hear?' Georgia whispered, ramming the bullet down the barrel and cocking the hammer.

Dakkar put a finger to his lips and pointed his other hand to the front door.

As if to answer Georgia's question, a sharp hissing echoed around the shadowy hall. She pulled back the hammer of her rifle and inched forward.

Dakkar's eyes widened as he realised that the hissing was continuous, not like the hissing of a snake ... more like the hissing of a fuse.

'It's a bomb!' he yelled.

Dakkar hurled himself at Georgia, bundling her

through the door of Oginski's study and landing in a heap on the carpet.

The roar of the explosion filled the hall, accompanied by the rending of wood and metal as the planks of the door crashed inwards, bounced across the hall and smashed into the table. Smoke and flame consumed the hallway.

CHAPTER SEVEN
INVASION!

The rumble of the explosion died, leaving a buzzing in Dakkar's ears. Muffled footsteps echoed in the gutted hall. Orders were shouted. Men hurried through the fog of brick dust and smoke – dressed in black uniform with the Cryptos emblem emblazoned on the shoulder.

'Tomasz's men!' Georgia whispered, scrambling to her feet and retrieving her rifle.

Dakkar leapt up after her, gripping her shoulder.

'Wait!' he hissed. 'If you run out there all guns blazing, you'll be dead in seconds!'

'What do *you* suggest?'

'This.' Dakkar grinned, producing another small clockwork dog. 'It's a flash bomb. It'll stun anyone in that hall and give us a chance to find Oginski. He can't have missed that explosion, no matter how busy he is down in the cave!'

Georgia nodded her agreement.

Dakkar wound the toy dog up, setting it on the floor. It

waddled out of Oginski's study and into the hall. The smoke and dust had begun to thin and Dakkar counted at least six men in the hall. One looked down as the dog approached.

'Cover your eyes and ears,' Dakkar said, ducking behind a sofa with Georgia.

'What the ...?' the guard began, but his words were lost in the second explosion.

Even with his eyes closed and his hands over his ears, Dakkar could hear the boom and see the flash. He blinked once and hurried out into the hall, followed by Georgia.

Men lay groaning on the floor, stunned by the blast of the explosives hidden in the toy dog.

'Clever.' Georgia grinned but then yelped as a rifle ball smacked into the wall right next to Dakkar.

More guards appeared at the wrecked doorway.

Georgia ran up the stairs on their right and Dakkar followed.

'Why did you come up here?' Dakkar said, chasing her two steps at a time.

'It's narrow and we have the advantage of height,' Georgia panted.

Dakkar glanced back. The guards peered cautiously after them.

'But we're trapped now!' he groaned, hurling his empty rifle down at the men.

A loud explosion above Dakkar and Georgia made them start. Together they ran up another flight of stairs, only to be met by more smoke.

'That came from the roof,' Georgia said. 'They've set fire to it!'

They stood on the second floor landing now, smoke billowing in from above and the Cryptos Guard shouting at the foot of the stairs. The men knew that Dakkar and Georgia had nowhere to run.

'Follow me,' Dakkar said, darting into his bedroom and over to the window.

The night was lit up by the blaze above them. Dakkar could see as if it were daylight. Black-clad guards hurried between the outhouses that dotted the tower's grounds. With a gasp, they noticed three balloons floating, pale and ghostly, in the sky. Something flared in one of the baskets and a streak of sparks shot from it.

'They're firing rockets into the tower,' Dakkar murmured. 'The castle will be a pile of rubble if we don't stop them.' Another blast shook the tower as he spoke. 'We have to get down!'

'Do you have any rope?' Georgia said, gripping his arm.

'Yes, I always keep a supply of rope hidden in my wardrobe for just such an eventuality,' Dakkar said, stepping away from the window.

'There's no need to be sarcastic,' Georgia began. 'I just thought that maybe –'

'I'm not being sarcastic,' Dakkar said, grinning despite the chaos that surrounded them. 'I do have some rope. It's long enough for us to get out of the window here. I used it all the time when I was younger – I was always running away from Oginski.'

He opened the wooden wardrobe and rummaged in the contents at the bottom, pulling out several boxes and, finally, a rope.

'There's ammunition in the small boxes there,' he said as he uncoiled the rope and tied one end to the bed. 'And another rifle. You give me covering fire as I descend then I'll cover you.'

'All right,' Georgia said, loading her rifle while Dakkar threw open the little window.

'It's a bit of a squeeze,' he grunted, climbing on to the sill. 'I'm a bit bigger than when I used to slide out of here in the middle of the night.'

The outhouses were on fire now and dark figures flitted between them. Another explosion lit up the night sky and punctuated the crackling and snapping that came from the blazing roof above.

Georgia passed him the rifle and the powder and shot in a small satchel. Dakkar gave her a grin and, gripping the rope with both hands, began to walk his way backward down the side of the castle. His heart pounded. *Nobody has spotted me yet but it's only a matter of time!*

No sooner had Dakkar thought this than a bullet smacked into the stone next to his shoulder. He looked down to see one of Tomasz's men reloading his musket. A shot from the window above sent the man slumping to the ground, clutching his arm.

Dakkar half slid and half fell down the remaining distance as a second guard raised his gun. Using his downward momentum, Dakkar released the rope and landed feet first on the guard's head, sending him sprawling to the ground, unconscious. He snatched up the man's rifle and spun round, scanning for any threats.

Georgia inched out of the window and began her descent. A rifle shot cracked beside to her, this time from a hot-air balloon that floated close to the blazing roof.

Raising the rifle to his shoulder, Dakkar aimed at the guard in the balloon's basket and fired. His shot missed but struck something else inside the basket. A tongue of flame leapt into the air and Dakkar could hear cries of alarm. The balloon began to lose height, drifting towards the roof of the castle.

Dakkar watched in horror as the balloon became engulfed in the inferno of the castle. Men screamed and jumped from the basket only to plummet to the hard ground.

'I didn't mean for that –' he began.

'No time, Dax,' Georgia said, landing beside him and grabbing his arm. 'We can get back into the castle through the kitchen door. Maybe we can sneak into the cave and get to Oginski.'

They hurried around the side of the tower and through the back door. The kitchen lay dark and cool. It was almost as if nothing was happening outside. The thick walls muffled the sounds but the acrid smoke scented the air and the spit and pop of guns and rockets still drifted in through the cracked windows.

'Quickly!' Georgia said.

They rushed for the door to Oginski's workshop and threw themselves inside.

Dakkar scanned the workshop. The familiar clutter of cogs, springs, levers and old plans all remained untouched but the door to the sea cave was open.

'They must still be down there,' Dakkar said and hurried off into the gloom.

'Frank? Is that you?' Borys stood, waiting by the side of the *Nautilus*.

'We're under attack,' Dakkar said. 'Where's Oginski?'

'He went looking for you when we heard the first explosions!' Borys said, his eyes wide. 'Didn't you see him?'

'You mean he's still up there?' Dakkar said, turning for the stairs.

'Dakkar, wait!' Georgia yelled, yanking him backward. 'You can't go back up there. It's too dangerous!'

'I can't leave Oginski on his own,' Dakkar said and shook her off.

A shrill screech brought him to a stop.

A humanoid creature about half Dakkar's height stood on the tower of the *Nautilus*. Spines covered its blue body and it stared with bulbous, milky eyes. It raised the barbed spear in its fist to hurl the weapon at them but Georgia raised her rifle first and blasted the creature off the craft.

With a scream and a fountain of black blood, it sank into the water.

'A Qalupalik,' Borys gasped.

'Well, whatever it was,' Georgia said, her voice low, 'its cousins are here too and they don't look pleased …'

More blue heads and cloudy eyes popped up from the surface of the pool that filled the cave. Some clambered out, gripping the rock platform with scaly, webbed fingers and blocking the route to the stairs. Others crept on to the front of the *Nautilus*, inching forward, spears at the ready.

'I fear we are outgunned and outnumbered,' Borys whispered.

CHAPTER EIGHT
DESPERATE MEASURES

Hissing with menace, the small, spiny Qalupalik edged forward, forcing Borys, Dakkar and Georgia to shuffle closer together. A crowd had emerged from the sea now, almost surrounding them.

'Our only hope is to get into the *Nautilus*,' Borys whispered. 'At least we can lock them out.'

'But what about Oginski?' Dakkar said through clenched teeth. 'He's trapped up there.'

'There are more of them blocking the stairs – you'd never cut your way through them,' Georgia said, holding him back. 'They may be small but those spears look deadly and there are just too many.'

'Very well,' Dakkar grunted. 'On my word, we make a dash for the *Nautilus*. Here.' He passed Borys the rifle he had taken from the guard at the foot of the tower. 'It's loaded. Choose your target carefully and make your shot count.'

'I will, my friend. I will,' Borys said, a tremor in his voice.

'Ready?' Dakkar said.

They all nodded.

'Now!'

Leaping back, Dakkar fired his rifle over the heads of the Qalupalik, winging one individual who stood on a higher outcrop of rock. Swinging his rifle like a scythe, he cleared a path to the submarine.

Borys fired, sending one of the nearest creatures tumbling back into the others. Several fell into the water. Georgia ran across the gangplank, clearing the bow of the *Nautilus* with her shot. The Qalupalik not caught by the bullets leapt back into the pool for safety.

Borys slipped a knife from the top of his boot and slashed at the mooring rope as he crossed the gangplank.

The deafening screech from the Qalupalik intensified and they rushed forward, a tide of spiky arms and legs. Dakkar swept at them from the gangplank as Borys and Georgia scrambled up the tower of the sub. But more came, grabbing at his ankles and pulling at his clothes. He began to overbalance.

Then the whole cavern shook. Rocks and stalactites tumbled from the ceiling, smashing into the water and sending the creatures scattering. A huge chunk of stone crashed down only inches from Dakkar, crushing one of the Qalupalik who held him. He turned away from the sickening pool of blood that seeped from under it. More rock rained down now, fists of stone punching at Dakkar's back and shoulders as he climbed up into the sub. Slamming the hatch behind him, he slid down into the tower and groaned in pain.

It was like being inside a drum. Stones hammered on the hollow craft. Georgia had already started the engine and steered away from the platform. Slowly they sank as she blew the air from the hollow hull of the *Nautilus*. Through the window, the water boiled and black blood fogged the view. Qalupalik pounded on the window, faces fixed in toothy scowls.

Borys grabbed the wheel on the wall in front of him and spun it round twenty times. This friction wheel generated an electric charge and had proved a powerful weapon in the past.

'Twenty turns, was it?' he snarled. 'I'll teach these little monsters to threaten us!'

He stabbed the red button next to the wheel and the water outside suddenly lit blue.

Dakkar peered out at the small, now limp forms that floated by and shuddered.

More rock from above punched down into the water, clipping the sub.

'The whole cave is collapsing,' Georgia yelled above the clatter. 'We have to get out into the open sea.'

'But Oginski is still in the castle,' Dakkar shouted, grabbing hold of her arm.

'We'll be buried alive if we stay here,' Borys said, dragging Dakkar back. 'We can help Frank once we're free of this rockfall!'

The *Nautilus* pitched and tossed as bigger pieces of rock tumbled down into the water. Georgia steered the submarine for the exit cave, veering to port or starboard as necessary to dodge debris that plummeted into the depths.

Scraping the sides against the walls of the exit, Georgia wrestled with the wheel as she fought the surge of water caused by falling stone. Dakkar flinched at the bumps and crashes that shook the craft. Stirred by the current, the glowing blue seaweed slapped at the sub's portholes. Slight figures flashed by them as some of the Qalupalik that had survived the electric shock tried to escape the rockfall.

A sudden burst from behind them washed the craft forward, making Dakkar's stomach lurch and knocking everyone off their feet. The cave had completely collapsed. Fragments of rock and strands of weed hurtled past them as they began to lose momentum. Georgia kept steering ahead until the water calmed.

'Turn around quickly!' Dakkar said, climbing to his feet. 'Let's find Oginski!'

'I fear we still have company,' Borys said ominously.

More of the Qalupalik floated in a line ahead of them, spears at the ready, but they held back.

'They're right to be wary,' Georgia said, narrowing her eyes. 'We'll run them down.'

'No – look,' Dakkar said, pointing outside.

Another group swam down into the murky depths and wrestled something open. Amid the silt, Dakkar glimpsed what looked like a cage door being opened. A large cage door.

Something sinewy and snake-like swam out of the cage, ignoring the creatures.

'The eel,' Georgia hissed. 'The Qalupalik were controlling it!'

They could see it clearly now – longer than the *Nautilus*, with green, mottled skin. Dakkar recognised those wild, staring eyes and the rows of razor teeth.

'Never in my life have I seen such a monster,' Borys said, grimacing. 'A truly horrible specimen.'

'I hate eels,' Dakkar said, slumping his shoulders. 'I hate big eels even more. Good job we'd loaded the Sea Arrows.'

'I'll keep dodging the darned thing until you're ready,' Georgia said, ramming the *Nautilus* to *Full Ahead*.

Dakkar and Borys hurried down the steps into the heart of the *Nautilus* and the forward cabin that housed the Sea Arrows and the firing devices.

'We haven't got time to waste with this eel,' Dakkar spat. 'Oginski is up in that castle on his own.'

'Then let's get this right first time,' Borys said grimly.

They ran to the boxes that contained the Sea Arrows and pulled out a missile each. Opening the chambers in either side of the craft, they slid the Sea Arrows in and pulled back the catches that loaded the powerful springs that would fire them.

'We're loaded, Georgia,' Dakkar said into the speaking tube. 'Don't waste these shots!'

'I can't see it! Where's it … Oh no!'

The sub shook and Dakkar felt weightless for a second. The floor rose up and he hit the ceiling, jarring his back. Then the floor came up to meet him. Pain seared through his cheek as he fell flat on to the hard planks. Then the breath was forced from his lungs as Borys landed on top of him.

'Georgia, what happened?' he said, gripping the speaking tube tightly.

'It's on our tail,' Georgia groaned. The craft shuddered again. 'It's ripping into the outer hull.'

'If it gets through we won't be able to surface!' Dakkar said, jumping to his feet. Another tremor shook the submarine. 'The friction wheel, Georgia!'

The blue flash of electricity outside the porthole told Dakkar that she had anticipated his idea. Dakkar held his breath. *Did it work?*

A groaning sound reverberated through the planks and Dakkar was thrown to one side again.

'It won't let go,' Georgia yelled.

Dakkar hurried through the submarine and up the steps. Georgia looked pale. She was cranking the friction wheel again and trying to steer the *Nautilus* at full speed at the same time. She jagged the wheel left and right, sending Dakkar lurching from side to side. Peering out of the rear tower window, he could just see the eel wriggling beneath their rudders.

'It must be clamped on to the lower hull of the sub,' Dakkar said.

'If it keeps biting into the hull, we're done for,' Borys said, mopping his brow with a handkerchief.

Dakkar saw the creature's body twist and the *Nautilus* juddered again, listing slightly.

'It's going to tear us apart,' he muttered, glancing down at a lever by Georgia's left foot. It ran into the pipes that snaked all over the *Nautilus*. He'd never seen it before. One of Borys and Oginski's new additions, no doubt. 'What does this do?' he said.

'That?' Borys said distractedly. 'It inflates the balloons, I think. I hardly see –'

'Surface – quickly!' Dakkar said.

'What's the use in that?' Georgia said, still wrestling with the wheel.

'Just do it,' Dakkar said. 'At least we can jump out if we're on the surface. Besides, I have a plan.'

'Jump out? With those savages in the water and this eel?' Borys said, but Georgia turned the ballast handle and bubbles began to boil around them.

They bobbed up to the surface, the sea lit with the blazing castle up on the cliff. Dakkar dragged the lever back. The *Nautilus* rocked again and he watched through the portholes as the balloons burst from their pods and began to inflate.

'What have you done?' Borys gasped.

'Taken desperate measures,' Dakkar said, grinning grimly and watching as the *Nautilus* changed into something new and untested.

CHAPTER NINE
THE JAWS OF DEFEAT

The balloons surrounding the *Nautilus* rose, becoming gas-filled clouds of silk and sail. The ropes attaching them to the craft tightened and gradually the craft began to tilt. Dakkar held his breath.

'The weight of that critter is holding us down,' Georgia exclaimed. 'the *Nautilus* will never get out of the water!'

The submarine shook again as the eel thrashed, gripping to the splintered hull with its razor teeth.

'We'll see,' Dakkar murmured, not taking his eyes off the writhing eel. They tilted upward now as the *Nautilus* hung half in, half out of the sea. He could see the exposed body of the eel churning the water around it.

'It might work,' Borys said calmly. 'I'll go and see to the furnace. Perhaps some extra hot air will help matters!' He struggled along the side of the cabin and slid carefully down the ladder.

Dakkar looked up at the balloons straining at the ropes

and the tubes leading to them. *I just hope it works*, he thought. *We've got to get Oginski!*

A hiss and a clanking through the craft told them that Borys had the furnace working. Slowly the balloons swelled even more. The cabin became uncomfortably warm. Sweat trickled off Dakkar's brow.

Then the stern of the submarine began to lift, the eel dangling from her, its teeth embedded in the hard planks of the hull.

'It's working!' Dakkar said, slapping his hand against the wall.

Slowly, they rose, the glimmer of the flames from the castle reflecting on the receding waves. They gained height and the eel's wriggling became more urgent. The whole craft swung from side to side on the ropes.

Borys rejoined them, stumbling as the *Nautilus* rocked. Below, Dakkar could see the tiny Qalupalik in the water, shaking their spears.

'Our invention works!' Borys said, grinning. 'The *Nautilus* is flying!'

'Yeah, but we still have an eel attached to our tail!' Georgia said sourly.

'It can't hang on for ever,' Dakkar said. 'It needs the water. It must let go soon.'

'Well, I wish it would hurry up and drop off,' Georgia grumbled. 'We could go up to the top of the tower and shoot it.'

'And if you hit one of the balloons by mistake?' Borys said, raising his eyebrows.

The eel thrashed about even more, throwing them around the cabin. Dakkar gripped the back of Georgia's chair and watched behind him as the eel let go suddenly.

Dakkar's stomach lurched as the craft swayed, righted herself and began to rise. He glimpsed the Qalupalik scattering below as the wriggling eel plummeted towards them and hit the sea with an explosive splash.

The *Nautilus* drifted closer to the cliff face.

'If you turn that valve there,' Borys said, pointing to a valve in the wall, 'you can release some of the gas and hot air from the balloons. That way we won't carry on rising. In theory.'

Dakkar turned the valve and was rewarded with distant hissing. He stopped it, nervous of venting too much gas.

Their ascent slowed down and the cliff face vanished as they rose over a scene of horror. Dakkar's heart thumped against his ribs as he looked at the blazing castle. This wasn't the first time that Cryptos had tried to destroy his home but it was still terrible to see. Explosions burst from the outhouses where fire had taken hold of the volatile ingredients of Oginski's various experiments. The castle had been blown in half and flames rose from the shell that survived.

Oginski stood at the top of what remained of the tower, blood soaking the sleeve of his left arm. In his right he held a sword and he parried the relentless blows of a huge man in black Cryptos uniform. The guard lunged at Oginski with his own sword. Oginski was a big man but this man was taller and stockier still.

'We must get out and try to save Oginski,' Dakkar said, snatching up a rifle. 'Borys, you take over from Georgia. Get the *Nautilus* as close to the wall as you can. We'll do the firing.'

Dakkar climbed up the ladder, not waiting for Georgia. They were so close now that the heat from the blaze hit him as he opened the hatch. Smoke filled the air, making them cough and splutter. The *Nautilus* swayed on her ropes as the thermal currents from the burning castle pushed her around.

Oginski looked pale and exhausted as he hacked back at the guard, who didn't seem to be tiring. Dakkar took aim at Oginski's opponent and fired. The submarine lurched at that moment, sending his shot wide. The guard's attention was drawn though and he stared at the floating submarine in disbelief. Oginski took the chance to slam the hilt of his sword into his opponent's face, knocking him off the narrow fragment of wall and down into the darkness below.

Dakkar grinned but a bullet zipped past his ear as two hot-air balloons drifted towards him, men aiming from the baskets.

Georgia popped her head up out of the tower and fired back, cutting through one of the ropes that held the basket to the balloon. The basket swung down, leaving the men gripping its tilting sides as it drifted away across the cliffs.

Oginski desperately parried blow after blow as more guards scrambled up the wall of the castle to attack him.

Dakkar cursed, firing a shot at the crowd, but more men edged their way to Oginski's other side.

'Dakkar!' Oginski yelled. 'Flee! Get away from here. There are too many of them. Save yourself!'

'Never,' Dakkar cried back. 'Not without you!'

The *Nautilus* swung nearer so that only a few feet lay between Oginski and Dakkar but the dark sea swirled and snapped at the bottom of the narrow chasm between them. Sweat streamed down the big man's face, mingling with the blood from cuts and minor wounds.

'Bring her closer!' Dakkar yelled down to Borys.

'I'm trying my best!' Borys shouted back.

Some of the men on the wall slashed out at the hull of the *Nautilus*.

'Oginski, jump!' Dakkar said, holding out his arms.

Oginski half turned then swung the hilt of his sword into a guard's face and stabbed another in the arm.

'Dakkar, look out!' he bellowed.

Another hot-air balloon loomed around the ruins, its bullets splintering the planks that partly sheltered Dakkar. The *Nautilus* swung back, carried on a sudden updraft caused by one of the outhouses collapsing in a shower of sparks, but the smaller, lighter Cryptos balloon flew straight at them, bumping its basket into the bow of the submarine.

A rope with a grappling iron swung from the basket and snagged the foot of the sub's ladder. Three men leapt on to the front deck of the *Nautilus*. Dakkar's ears rang as Georgia fired her rifle over his shoulder. He saw one of the men fall to the deck, clutching his shoulder, but as the craft pitched with the new weight, he slid and fell, screaming to the sea below.

The second guard rushed forward and tried to scramble up the ladder to the top of the sub's tower. Dakkar waited for him to get closer then jabbed with the butt of his rifle. The man slipped back and pulled a pistol from his belt. Dakkar hurled himself back as the pistol roared. His momentum threw him into Georgia, who was about to shoot at the third man on the deck.

Seeing his chance, the guard on the ladder clambered on to the top of the tower and stood triumphantly over Dakkar. Borys appeared at the hatch into the tower. He flicked his hand and the guard looked down in disbelief as the handle of a knife appeared in his stomach. Borys lunged forward and grabbed the handle, retrieving his blade and pushing the man off the sub at the same time. Dakkar shuddered at Borys's cruel grin.

Georgia had scrambled to her feet and snatched up Dakkar's rifle. She took aim at the final man on the deck and clipped his ankle, sending him limping back to the basket of the Cryptos balloon. He threw himself over the lip of the basket and untied the rope that held the two together. Slowly the Cryptos balloon separated from the *Nautilus*.

A metallic clicking sound caught Dakkar's attention and he looked at Borys, who was busy winding something.

'I modified one of your little toys,' he said, holding up the clockwork dog that he had picked up from his workbench days ago.

Borys gave a chilling laugh and threw the dog after the retreating balloon. It landed in the centre of the basket.

'Not a bad throw, if I say so myself.' Borys nodded, watching the man in the balloon frantically trying to find the missile.

The balloon erupted in a flash of light and fire. Dakkar threw his arms up to cover his eyes and then turned on Borys.

'There was no need for that!' he said. 'The balloon was retreating.'

'This is no time to be squeamish, Dakkar,' Borys said, returning to the hatch. 'Now I'd better get back to the helm. We're drifting.'

Dakkar spun back to the melee on the shattered castle wall. Oginski had cleared the knot of men behind him but a larger tangle of armed guards pushed at him, jabbing with bayonet and sword. Luckily for Oginski, the narrow wall would only allow his opponents to stand two abreast, making their numbers irrelevant. Oginski used their ungainly jostling to overbalance and trip the guards but they were overwhelming him.

The *Nautilus* swung back, grinding against the rough stone. Oginski glanced at Dakkar and pushed the man in front of him heavily in the chest, which sent him stumbling back into the crowd behind him.

Without hesitating, Oginski leapt from the wall. For a moment, he seemed frozen in mid-air, hovering almost, his jacket tails flowing out like strange wings and his arms held high. Dakkar held his breath. Then Oginski hit the side of the *Nautilus* with a loud *thump*, his fingers grappling at the various handholds that dotted the craft's hull.

'He's made it!' Georgia screamed. 'Borys, draw away quickly, before …'

But Georgia's instructions turned into a scream. A musket cracked, spitting from the wall. Oginski's eyes widened and a trickle of blood ran down his chin.

'*Oginski!*' Dakkar howled, leaping down the tower on to the deck of the *Nautilus*. He scrambled towards the side of the craft where Oginski hung, gasping for breath.

'Dakkar,' he panted, looking up with heavy eyes. 'Find the Heart of Vulcan. Stop Tomasz.'

'Oginski, no!' Dakkar reached down to grab his hand.

'I'm … p-proud … of you,' Oginski said, giving a bloody grin, and his grip on the *Nautilus* slackened. Dakkar lunged forward but his mentor slid off the side of the *Nautilus* and vanished into the roaring darkness below.

CHAPTER TEN

A RACE FOR REVENGE

'Oginski!' Dakkar screamed, launching himself forward, but Georgia grabbed hold of him and Borys dragged him to the floor.

Dakkar stared down into the swirling shadows at the foot of the cliff in mute disbelief. The gap between the cliff and the unpiloted *Nautilus* widened as the craft drifted away.

A bullet whacked into the woodwork next to Dakkar, snapping him out of his nightmare. Borys and Georgia still clung on to him. Dakkar kicked and punched, desperate to get free.

More gunfire cracked as the guards focused their attention on the submarine now that Oginski was gone.

'Stop!' Georgia yelled, gripping Dakkar's face in her hands and staring into his eyes. 'There's nothing you can do. He's gone. We have to escape!'

'I'll kill them,' Dakkar screamed. 'Let me go!'

More guards charged to the cliff edge and formed a line, pointing their rifles.

'Georgia!' Borys shouted. 'We need to leave. Go and steer us away. Now!'

Georgia vanished down into the *Nautilus*. The sound of gas hissing into the balloons drowned out the roar of the sea and the flames and suddenly the craft rose high into the air. Bullets whirred around them, some smacking into the hull.

'No!' Dakkar yelled, lunging forward again.

This time, Borys's firm hand clamped a damp cloth around Dakkar's mouth and nose, engulfing him in a sour smell. Then darkness invaded his vision. The spit of gunfire grew faint and all was black.

Visions of Oginski falling tormented Dakkar's dreams. Time and again he leapt, trying to catch his mentor, only to fail and see him tumbling to the waves below.

Oginski's voice would whisper from the raging waters. 'Men are so consumed by revenge they become monsters,' it said. 'Are you a monster?'

And then it was Dakkar falling, plunging down into a raging sea of blood.

Dakkar woke with a start.

'Whoa!' Georgia said, placing a soft hand on his shoulder. 'You've had a bad dream.'

He glanced around. They were in his cabin in the *Nautilus*. The engine hummed and, from the pitch and roll of the craft, he couldn't tell whether they were in the air or underwater.

Georgia smiled at him, her eyes red and puffy with crying.

'What happened?' he said, groaning and rubbing his head.

'Borys knocked you out with some kind of sleeping potion on a handkerchief,' Georgia said. 'You were all for jumping over the side of the *Nautilus* to your death …' She gave a choking cough and fought back more tears.

'I wanted to save Oginski,' Dakkar said. He felt numb, guilty at not shedding tears for his mentor. 'We should go back. He might have survived …'

Georgia shook her head sadly. 'Nobody could survive a fall like that,' she said, sniffing back a tear.

The cabin door swung open and Borys popped his head in. He looked pale and sombre.

'You're awake – good,' he said and gave a sigh. 'My apologies for the way I subdued you but it was for your own good. The potion is something Tomasz and I concocted from certain types of seaweed. Harmless in small quantities. The headache will pass.'

'Where are we going?' Dakkar said, rubbing his temples.

'That is up to you,' Borys said with a slight shrug. 'Personally, I went to stop my brother from conquering the world. But maybe Franciszek's peace-loving philosophy has taken away your stomach for vengeance …'

'You underestimate me.' Dakkar looked hard at Oginski's brother.

Borys stepped into the tiny room and leaned close, placing a hand on Dakkar's shoulder. 'My brother taught you well enough to be resourceful without him,' Borys said in a low voice. 'But this is Tomasz we're talking about. He's a wily adversary.'

Dakkar felt a wave of anger. 'I'm not afraid of him,' he said through gritted teeth. 'We're going to find the Heart of Vulcan. Then I'm going to stop Tomasz. It was the last thing Oginski told me to do.'

'You think you're a match for Tomasz?' Borys raised an eyebrow. 'I'm impressed. With an anger like that burning inside you, who knows?'

'*I* know,' Dakkar said, clenching his fists.

'Good lad.' Borys grinned, patting Dakkar's cheek. 'Keep that fire burning! Now, we must not dwell on the past. There'll be time for grieving later but now things need to be done. This is a race for revenge!'

'It's a race to find the Thermolith,' Georgia said, her arms folded and a guarded expression on her face. 'And to save the world.'

'Whether it's revenge or a nobler cause, we'll have to reckon with Tomasz sooner or later,' Borys said, balancing his hands as if he were the Scales of Justice. 'Maybe we can end his reign of terror before it begins. Rouse yourself, Dakkar – there is much to be done!' He walked out of the cabin before either Dakkar or Georgia could question what he had just said.

Dakkar climbed out of the small bed and stretched, his knuckles grazing either wall of the room. He looked across at Georgia, who stood, arms still folded.

'So is that what it is? A race for revenge?' Georgia said.

She looked small and alone. Dakkar wanted to reach out to her but cold fury still seethed in his belly.

'We must find the Thermolith,' he said. 'But I *will* make Tomasz pay for … what he did.' Dakkar still couldn't say out loud that Oginski was dead.

'Borys sounded like the first Oginski brother we met, Kazmer,' Georgia said. 'He wanted you to be a monster.'

'*Are you a monster?*' Oginski's words echoed through his mind. But Oginski wasn't here now.

Dakkar shrugged. 'Come on,' he said. 'Let's go and see what needs doing.'

Borys sat at the controls of the *Nautilus*, making Dakkar clench his teeth. He stood close to the round man until Borys looked up at him.

'You want to captain for a while?' Borys said, his face a picture of innocence.

'The *Nautilus* is mine,' Dakkar said darkly, sliding into the captain's seat as Borys vacated it.

'I think you'll find it belonged to the late Franciszek Oginski,' Borys said quietly. 'And, as his next of kin …'

'The *Nautilus* is mine,' Dakkar repeated through gritted teeth.

'Very well, my prince,' Borys said, a tight smile on his face. 'So, tell me, what's the plan? Do you know where you're going?' He folded his arms and leant back against the wall of the control room.

The room felt very crowded. Dakkar's face flushed red.

'You have a map,' he muttered, not meeting Borys's eye. 'I'll use that.'

'You saw the map,' Borys said. 'It was drawn in haste. But I have contacts who can guide us to the Thermolith. You need me, Dakkar.'

'Very well,' Dakkar said, throwing himself back in the seat. 'What do you advise then?'

'We fly as far as we can towards Greenland,' Borys said. 'When it becomes too cold for the balloons and we lose too much altitude, we shall take to the water.'

'And once we're in Greenland?' Georgia said.

'I have a contact in Guthaven in the west. An Inuit hunter called Tingenek,' Borys said. 'We'll find him and prepare for the mission.'

'Are you certain this Tingenek can help us?' Dakkar said.

'As certain as I can be,' Borys said. 'Tingenek is fond of drink, and quarrelsome, but he knows the land better than we ever could. He'll be able to guide us. In the meantime,' he added, 'we need to be able to trust each other. You can't pilot the craft all the time. Besides, certain repairs need to be carried out ...'

Dakkar clung to the hull of the *Nautilus*, screwing his eyes against the cold wind that stung his face. When they had first taken flight in the dark, he hadn't had time to marvel at the view from this height. Now he tried not to stare down at the endless grey and white waves that rose and fell so far below. He looked over to Georgia, who seemed equally unhappy about where she stood at that moment.

'Do we really need to be out here?' she yelled above the gale.

'There's a lot of damage to the underside of the craft,' Dakkar replied in an equally loud voice. 'We need a dry dock to carry out full repairs but we don't have the luxury of time.'

They inched along the *Nautilus*, tying ropes to the grab handles and mooring points that studded her rear deck. Not daring to look down, Dakkar focused his attention on the knots that were becoming harder to tie as his fingers became colder.

Georgia worked deftly and quickly had more rope secure than Dakkar as they shifted along the sub.

'Hurry up! I'm freezing, waiting for you,' she said, giving a tight smile.

Dakkar grinned back and immediately felt guilty as the image of Oginski falling invaded his mind.

Gradually, they built a web of ropes that criss-crossed the planks of the craft, giving them something to cling on to as they moved around. Dakkar's confidence grew and he allowed himself a glimpse over the side. His stomach lurched. Ever since he'd ridden on the back of a giant flying reptile in the underground world ruled by Stefan Oginski, Dakkar had not liked heights.

They picked out musket balls lodged in the wood and filled the holes left behind with hot tar. There was little chance for conversation in the battering winds. Clambering around the network of ropes holding on to a bucket of hot tar was tricky. Dakkar concentrated on digging the lead shot out, forcing his mind to be still and free from thoughts of Oginski.

Glancing down again, he noticed a dark patch drifting in the sea. At first he thought it was the shadow of a cloud on the surface. Peering hard, however, Dakkar could see that it was under the water.

Could it be the eel that attacked us at the castle? He shook his head. *No – this shape is too big. Whatever it is, it must be massive to be visible at this height.*

The shape seemed to move with the *Nautilus*, tracking them. Dakkar couldn't help feeling that danger was stalking them far below.

CHAPTER ELEVEN
MY ENEMY'S ENEMY

The days wore on and the steel seas seemed endless. Dakkar wondered at how relentless and dull the water could be.

The shadow still drifted along in their wake. Dakkar pointed it out to Borys, who merely shrugged.

'It's too big to be the eel. It could be the shadow of the *Nautilus* herself!' Borys said, craning his neck to peer out of the window. 'Or maybe a shoal of herring.' He licked his lips. 'Actually, that's making me hungry!'

Food was an issue. Their hasty departure meant that nothing more than a few dry rations had been stowed on board and certainly not enough for three people for over a week. Borys pulled terrible faces whenever he ate dinner, which was comprised of a few strips of salt beef and dry biscuits as hard as stone.

'Who put this muck in the supply cupboard?' he would grumble. 'What I wouldn't give for a decent glass of wine and a leg of roast duck!'

They took shifts at steering the sub and Dakkar began to relax a little when Borys took the helm. While one steered, the others would sleep or eat.

'I don't feel safe sleeping while Borys is steering,' Georgia said to Dakkar one day while Borys was asleep. 'He's still an Oginski.'

'I don't completely trust him,' Dakkar said, folding his arms. 'But I'll side with anyone who can help me find the Heart of Vulcan and stop Tomasz.'

'My enemy's enemy is my friend,' Georgia said sadly. 'And don't forget that I want to find this thing too. It isn't *me* – it's *us*.'

'Sorry,' Dakkar said, rubbing his eye with the heel of his hand. 'But someone has to pay for what happened.'

'Do they?' Georgia said. 'Do you think Oginski would want you to be hell-bent on revenge?'

'Maybe not,' Dakkar agreed, staring out of the window. 'But he told me to find the Thermolith and stop Tomasz.'

'There's a difference between stopping Tomasz and killing him,' Georgia said. 'Just don't let that temper of yours get in the way.'

'My temper?'

'You heard,' Georgia snapped. 'We need cool heads if we're to accomplish this mission.'

'I can control my temper,' Dakkar said and scrambled down into the belly of the *Nautilus* before Georgia could reply.

The *Nautilus* began to lose height. It was so gradual that it was hard to tell at first but Dakkar started to see the foamy crests of the waves more clearly and noticed the occasional pod of dolphins splashing by. The shadow that had dogged them for days wasn't anywhere to be seen.

Followed closely by Georgia, Dakkar hurried up to the helm to find Borys sitting there.

'The air is becoming colder,' Borys said, nodding out of the window.

Dakkar peered out to see the balloons looking baggy and loose.

'Now that it's colder outside, the hot air cools by the time it reaches the balloons,' Dakkar said, wiping his condensed breath from the glass.

'You are a clever young man,' Borys said, nodding. 'We'll save the gas. We have precious little anyway – it's so difficult to store. Soon we'll land and take to the waves.'

Dakkar wondered if 'land' was the correct word if they were surrounded by sea.

'Then we'll see if your furnace heats the submarine,' Dakkar said, warming his hands on the pipes that ran around the cabin.

'I hope so!' Borys said. 'The waters around Greenland are freezing cold. They would make life in the *Nautilus* even more uncomfortable.'

Dakkar watched the sea come ever closer then heard waves bumping against the hull.

'Hold on to something,' Borys called out. 'We're about to set down in the water.'

CHAPTER TWELVE
DANGER ISLAND

The waves rushed past, hissing against the sides of the *Nautilus*. The whole sub rocked and Dakkar and Georgia gripped the back of Borys's chair tightly. With a loud thump, the *Nautilus* hit the waves and began to roll with the tide.

'There,' Borys said. 'Expertly done, if I say so myself.'

Dakkar couldn't help but grin. 'We should gather in the balloons,' he said. 'Perhaps we could moor on that small islet.'

'What small islet?' Georgia said, frowning.

'There.' Dakkar pointed out of the window. Some distance away, the waves splashed on a small outcrop of rock.

'I didn't notice that on my descent,' Borys said, scratching his ear. 'But it would be good to stand on some solid ground after so many days at sea.'

He steered the *Nautilus* towards the islet. Dakkar climbed out on to the bow of the sub, rope in hand. As they drew nearer, it struck Dakkar that it was quite a large stretch of land. It looked as if a giant had dumped a huge pile of stones into the sea. Boulders and spikes of rock, crusted in barnacles and limpets, poked out of the thick seaweed that hung limply everywhere. He tied a loop in one end of the rope and managed to snag it on one of the stone slabs.

Borys appeared at Dakkar's shoulder. 'I don't remember this on any of the charts,' Borys said.

'Perhaps the tide is low and has uncovered the islet – it could be underwater most of the time,' Dakkar said, jumping off the *Nautilus* and on to the nearest rock. The ground felt solid under his feet.

'You don't look very happy to be on dry land,' Borys muttered, sounding surprised.

'The safety of land is an illusion,' Dakkar said darkly, taking a breath. 'At least at sea I can live freely.'

Borys joined him with an awkward jump, stumbling and soaking his shoes. 'At least land is generally dry,' he said, shaking a soggy foot. 'I'd sooner fly if I could.'

They wandered around the islet, picking their way over pools and slipping on the wet, seaweed-covered rock. Dakkar felt tiny and insignificant, encircled by miles and miles of grey water in all directions. A small sandy clearing sat in the island's centre, surrounded by the stone outcrops.

'It looks like some kind of crater,' Dakkar said, scraping his foot on the sand. 'Maybe it's the tip of a volcano.'

'Quite possibly,' Borys said. 'This clearing is sheltered from the wind. It would be good to make a fire and cook some fish or maybe a seabird.' He pulled out a handkerchief and dabbed his lips as if he had already eaten.

'Do we have time to spend?' Dakkar said, frowning.

'There is always time for good food,' Borys said, grinning. 'Besides, our supplies are dangerously low. We can stock up. What a stroke of luck, this island being here!'

Soon Dakkar and Georgia were busy setting up fishing lines while Borys fussed around, lighting a fire and trying to make a spit on which to turn the two fat seagulls he had snared easily with some salt beef as bait.

'There are plenty of fish down there,' Dakkar said, gazing down into the clear waters that surrounded the island. 'We shouldn't have much of a problem catching them.'

As if in answer to Dakkar's statement, one of the lines went taut, then another.

Georgia laughed. 'I bet there isn't any land for hundreds of miles in any direction,' she said. 'They must be drawn here for food.'

'A bit like him.' Dakkar nodded towards Borys as he clapped his hands, celebrating the sight of the birds turning over the flames.

Georgia smirked.

Dakkar drew fish after fish out of the water. Some they left by the fire for Borys to cook, the rest they took down to the engine room where they had set up a line for them to hang and dry out.

The afternoon rolled on. Dakkar lay by the fire, savouring the taste of roast seagull and fish.

'So you are a younger brother to ... my ... Oginski?' Dakkar swallowed down the upsurge of sorrow that came with the name.

'Did Franciszek not explain who we all are?' Borys said, his voice thick with gravy from the bird. 'Marek is the eldest, then ... your Oginski – Franciszek, then Voychek ... then us.'

'I see,' Dakkar said.

'Then Kazmer and Stefan,' Borys finished.

Georgia threw a hot piece of fish from palm to palm, trying to cool it. 'And where are Marek and Voychek?'

'Marek is in Africa,' Borys said. 'He's a bull in a china shop. A monster of a man. Bigger than Frank.'

'And Voychek?'

Borys paled and looked solemn. 'I haven't seen Voychek for many a year.' He shivered. 'At least, I don't think I have. I probably wouldn't recognise him if I did meet him.'

'What do you mean?' Dakkar suddenly felt chilly and shuffled nearer the fire.

'Voychek is a master of disguise,' Borys said with a haunted look in his eye. 'A shadow, a rumour these days. He's wild and unpredictable. Of all my brothers, it's he I fear most.'

'Then I sure hope we don't meet him,' Georgia said.

'Well, he's not here,' Borys said, shaking himself and trying to lift the sombre mood that had fallen over them. 'And we have good food.'

'You do like your food, Borys,' Dakkar said, giving a slight smile.

'If we weren't caught up with our brothers and their mad schemes,' Borys said, stifling a belch, 'Tomasz and I would have been the greatest chefs known to man. In fact, I still harbour a desire to conquer the so-called civilised nations of the world, if only to bring them decent food and wine!'

Borys roared with laughter but Dakkar just stared into the fire. Georgia glanced at Borys.

'How can you be so merry at a time like this?' she said.

'We have food in our bellies and a fire warming our toes, young lady,' Borys said mildly. 'There have been times when I have gone without and shivered with bone-biting cold, expecting the next breath to be my last. That's how I can be merry.'

'But Oginski …' she began.

Borys's face hardened. 'Revenge is the best poultice for that wound,' he said in a low voice. 'Right now we can't do anything about that but our time will come. Tomorrow we set off on our quest again. Tonight we rest. Franciszek wouldn't begrudge us that.'

Dakkar jumped up and stalked off to the furthest end of the islet.

'Leave him, Georgia,' he heard Borys say as he left. 'Let him grieve.'

The wind whipped at Dakkar's thick, black hair and chilled his face as he sat on the rocks staring out to sea.

Why don't I feel sad? Why do I just feel angry? he wondered. He thought of Oginski's weary face as he slipped to his death. Dakkar wanted to scream and shout, to punch something or someone.

A huge explosion of bubbles erupted at his feet, making him yell and leap back. Suddenly the ground beneath him shifted, sending him rolling towards the sea. He slapped his hand on to the slick rock, just breaking his fall, and hung there as the islet began to move.

'It's an earthquake!' he shouted to the others, who clung to nearby rocks, looking around in confusion.

The fire had scattered and Borys hastily snatched at the fish hanging over the embers, hissing and yelping as they burned his fingers.

'No time for that,' Georgia said, grabbing the man's sleeve. 'We've gotta get back to the *Nautilus*.'

The whole surface of the ground tilted, sending them tumbling into each other. Then it veered the other way.

'I've never known anything like it!' Borys panted, struggling to his feet.

'Neither have I,' Dakkar muttered, staring straight ahead, his heart hammering at his ribs.

The sea exploded in front of him in a fountain of white spray. An enormous column of green rock burst from the waves, rearing up above and sending water raining down on them.

'What is that?' Georgia whispered.

'It's a head,' Dakkar replied faintly.

Two cold, reptilian eyes cracked open and stared at them – from what was now clearly the neck and head of the biggest turtle Dakkar had ever seen. It peered down on them over its shoulder as they stood on what he assumed was its gargantuan shell. It opened its colossal beaked mouth and gave a shrieking roar.

Borys gaped at the beast. 'It's enormous,' he said.

'And it doesn't look happy!' Georgia added in a small, trembling voice.

CHAPTER THIRTEEN

A NANTUCKET SLEIGH RIDE

For a second, Dakkar could only stand and stare at the head that towered over him. The sound of its cry deafened him.

Borys gripped his arm and mouthed something but the monster's scream drowned out the words. Pale and wide-eyed, Borys pointed to the *Nautilus*, which bucked and reared, still tied to the creature's spiny carapace.

'We must get into the sub,' Borys repeated. 'This creature is going to submerge!'

Dakkar leapt forward, his feet splashing in puddles that were forming as water rushed over the side of the shell. Ahead he saw Georgia leaping on to the *Nautilus* and scrambling up the ladder. Borys wasn't far behind her.

'The hatch is open,' Dakkar called to them, slipping in the deepening waters. 'If the turtle sinks before we get in, the *Nautilus* will flood!'

The sub pointed nose-down in the water now as the

creature prepared to dive. Gasping in the freezing water, Dakkar found himself swimming to the tower. Something flashed beneath Dakkar and he glimpsed a milky eye and a downturned mouth.

'Qalupalik!' he yelled, kicking out at a scaly hand that tried to close around his ankle.

'Hurry, boy!' Borys yelled.

The *Nautilus* listed horribly now, the tower almost level with the sea. More of the screeching creatures appeared in the water. Spears splashed close to Dakkar and rattled against the hull of the *Nautilus*.

'They must have herded this thing towards us!' Dakkar said.

'Shut up and swim!' Borys said, ducking as another spear bounced off the woodwork.

Dakkar threw himself forward and scrambled towards the tower. Two Qalupalik leapt in his path. He kicked the legs from under one and smashed his fist into the other's face, sending it tumbling into its comrades. Without looking back, Dakkar leapt up the tower, slamming the hatch closed behind him.

'Did you untie the *Nautilus*?' Georgia called to them.

'I didn't have time,' Dakkar spluttered, shivering and wet. 'It's crawling with those little creatures out there!'

Water foamed all around them as the huge turtle sank beneath the waves. Angry faces glowered at them through the portholes. Dakkar could hear the thumps and bangs as the Qalupalik hammered at the hull of the sub.

'Looks like we're in for the Nantucket sleigh ride of all time,' Borys chuckled.

'The what?' Dakkar said.

'Nantucket sleigh ride,' Georgia said. She had settled herself into the captain's seat and was wrestling with the wheel as the huge turtle powered down into the sea. 'When whaler-men first harpoon a whale and it drags their ship along, that's what they call it.'

As if to demonstrate, the whole sub jerked, sending them staggering against the walls. The Qalupalik outside vanished suddenly.

'Here we go!' Borys yelled.

The vast bulk of the giant turtle filled the portholes of the *Nautilus* and bubbles of air blasted around the sub, making visibility poor. Fish and debris smacked against the hull of the craft as they careered after the creature, swaying from side to side on the rope. The Qalupalik had been left far behind.

Dakkar's stomach lurched and his ears popped as they plunged deeper into dark cold water.

'It is an amazing creature,' Borys said, squinting through the porthole. 'I never would have thought such a beast could exist.'

'My uncle used to tell me stories of the aspidochelone,' Georgia said, her head shaking in disbelief. 'A huge sea creature that drags unfortunate sailors and their ships down to the deepest depths after tricking them to land on its back.'

They powered through the water at an incredible rate, faster than even the *Nautilus* would normally go. Something heavy cracked against the hull of the sub, making Dakkar flinch.

'Well, we can't just sit here being dragged along by it,' he said. 'We have to cut ourselves free somehow.'

'We could blast the beast with a Sea Arrow,' Borys suggested. 'From the size of it, I doubt it would feel a thing but it may break us free.'

'We'd blow ourselves up,' Dakkar said, frowning. 'We're tied too close to the creature's shell, remember.'

'Could you swim out there?' Borys said. 'And cut the rope?'

Dakkar shuddered. 'We're moving too fast – I'd be ripped away from the sub and left far behind.'

'If we can't come up for air eventually, we'll suffocate down here,' Georgia said in a quiet voice.

Long minutes of silence ran on as each of them struggled to think of a way to cut free from the giant that was dragging them to their doom.

'What if we put the *Nautilus* into reverse?' Georgia suggested suddenly, making Dakkar jump.

'We'd be no match for a monster like this!' Borys snorted. 'How could we fight its massive strength?'

'We don't have to!' Dakkar grinned. 'Georgia, you're a wonder!'

'I don't understand,' Borys said with a frown.

'Sometimes the simplest solution is the best one.' Georgia grinned. 'We can just snap the rope. Hold on tight!' She slammed the drive lever to *Backwater* and the engines began to whine.

The whole sub shook as she tried to battle the relentless pull of the massive turtle but something seemed to be aiding them too.

'The drag as we're pulled along will be in our favour,' Dakkar said, peering through the darkness of the water. He could just see the vague outline of the rope, taut and quivering as the *Nautilus* tried to resist the journey of the monster.

Seaweed and dead fish smacked into the portholes and against the sub as she shuddered. Her engines screamed down below as Georgia pushed the sub to her limit.

The *Nautilus* began to veer more violently from side to side as she struggled to free herself of the mooring line that linked her to the turtle's shell. With a *twang*, the rope snapped. The sub spun sideways, sending everyone inside hurtling around the cabin. Dakkar found himself flat on his stomach, staring down the hatch into the *Nautilus*, gasping for breath.

Georgia sat in the captain's seat, gritting her teeth and heaving at the wheel, trying to regain control as they whirled through the water like a boomerang. Planks groaned and Dakkar heard supplies clattering from their storage cupboards down below.

Gradually the *Nautilus* stopped turning and Georgia, panting, brushed the hair from her face and gave a grin.

'Did it,' she said.

Before Dakkar could answer, the chilling shriek of the turtle cut through the water, filling the sub.

'It's turning round,' Dakkar said, staring out of the window.

The turtle's momentum had carried it into the far distance but it still looked colossal. Dakkar could make out its spiny shell and four massive flippers that pounded the water.

'Do we stand and fight?' Dakkar wondered aloud.

'With what?' Georgia murmured. 'Our Sea Arrows would barely scratch that thing's armour. No, we gotta hide!'

'Take the *Nautilus* as deep as you can,' Borys said. 'Try to find a reef or rocks to conceal us.'

'But too deep and the sheer weight of the water will crush us,' Dakkar whispered.

'I can't see we have much choice,' Georgia said, pursing her lips and steering the *Nautilus* downward.

The turtle gave another shriek. It sounded louder – as if it were gaining on them. Dakkar peered out – it looked larger, closer.

The darkness of the water closed in around them as they plunged deeper.

'We have to keep quiet,' Borys said, his voice low. 'Sound travels in water and I believe that our big friend's keepers, the Qalupalik, have very keen senses!'

Once more the planks of the *Nautilus* groaned with the pressure of the water. Dakkar felt a tightness around his chest and each breath seemed to pant from his body as if squeezed out.

Rocky pillars appeared out of the gloom. Georgia steered towards them and settled the *Nautilus* between them, shutting the engine down. Slowly the sub sank to the gritty seabed, hitting the ground with a thump that echoed dully through the whole craft.

They all waited in the cabin. Sweat dripped down Dakkar's forehead and neck as he peered out into the silty water. The heat was stifling. A huge shadow drifted above them. Dakkar pointed upward to tell the others. Georgia held her hand to her mouth.

Dakkar could hear the blood pulsing in his neck and his breath rasping in his lungs. The sea pressed in on the *Nautilus*'s timbers, making her creak. Every noise brought a wince from Dakkar. His jaw ached from gritting his teeth and he longed to scream out and send the *Nautilus* rushing to the surface.

The light from the surface above them darkened again.

The monster is circling, Dakkar thought. *It's searching for us like some kind of bloodhound!*

The silence pressed in on them. The air became stale and Dakkar's head pounded.

We can't wait much longer, he thought.

'What if we fire a couple of Sea Arrows,' he whispered, 'to create a distraction?'

'Good idea,' Georgia hissed back. 'If it kicks up enough mud, we can slip away unnoticed.'

'We could use sepia bombs too,' Dakkar said. 'To add to the confusion.'

In addition to the Sea Arrows, the *Nautilus* could fire globes of squid ink into the sea. These created a thick and slightly acidic fog through which the sub might be able to escape. Signalling Borys to go to the stern of the boat where the sepia bombs were kept, Dakkar climbed down the ladder and crept towards the cabin that housed the

Sea Arrows. He eased the explosive missiles out of their box and slid them into the firing chambers which nestled in the walls on either side of the sub.

'Dakkar?' Georgia's voice from the speaking tube made him jump. 'Are you ready?'

'Yes!' Dakkar hissed back. 'Keep quiet, will you?'

'No need for that now,' she replied. 'It's seen us and it's coming our way. Get ready!'

CHAPTER FOURTEEN
A FROZEN WORLD

Dakkar felt the *Nautilus* lift as Georgia blew some of the ballast water from the hull. He stabbed his thumb into the firing button and then into the second one. Two missiles sprang from the front of the sub. Dakkar waited and after a count of eight was rewarded with the dull thump of an explosion, followed closely by another.

He could tell that the *Nautilus* was travelling backward and he hurried up the passage and climbed the ladder back to the tower.

A thick fog of sepia and mud blotted out the view from inside the tower. Georgia had spun the *Nautilus* around and slammed her to *Full Ahead*. The shrieks of the turtle seemed more distant now.

'The Sea Arrows have deafened it,' Borys said, smiling grimly. 'I think we might have given it the slip.'

'Let's get to the surface,' Dakkar said. 'I need fresh air.' He felt sick and his head thumped.

Slowly, they rose through the murk, glad of the weak daylight that shone at the surface of the sea. They broke the waves and Dakkar gave a sigh of relief as he felt the sub pitch and roll.

They all clambered up the tower, eager to get their lungs full of clean air. Dakkar gasped at the sharpness of the cold that hit him as he threw open the hatch. He blinked, trying to adjust to the sudden bright light.

'What on earth?' Georgia whispered beside him.

Towering mountains of ice surrounded them, smaller ones rising and falling with the sea. Flat ice floes, broken into chunks, clunked against the wooden hull of the *Nautilus*. A cold wind moaned over this desolate scene.

'The beast must have dragged us further north than we thought,' Borys said, shivering. 'In all the excitement, I didn't even notice.'

'It's beautiful,' Georgia said, her breath clouding her face.

'It's too cold,' Dakkar muttered, shaking himself.

'Come back down into the *Nautilus*,' Borys said, putting an arm around Georgia. 'The cold is dangerous. You have to treat it with respect. Stay up here too long without protection and you will surely die.'

The warmth of the sub welcomed Dakkar as he slid down the ladder back inside. Borys looked grimly out of the porthole at the white crust that covered the sea's surface.

'This is bad,' he said and pursed his lips.

'But surely all we need to do is set a course further south and we can pick up our original course,' Dakkar said.

'It's not that easy, Dakkar,' Borys said. 'The turtle brought us deep under the ice floes and we must navigate back out of them. It's late in the year so the floes are beginning to thicken and freeze together. We might not be able to break through them.'

'But we can go under them,' Georgia said. 'That's how we got here.'

'This is true,' Borys agreed. 'But what if we can't surface because of the ice? What if we lose our way? There can be no navigation errors in the Arctic.'

They climbed down into the body of the *Nautilus* and went into the front cabin to consult the charts.

'By my calculations we're here,' Borys said, stabbing the compasses into the map at a point west of Greenland.

'How can that be?' Dakkar wondered. 'We weren't dragged for that long surely?'

'That creature is huge and powerful,' Borys said, tracing a finger over their supposed route. 'One stroke of its mighty flippers would be enough to propel us a great distance.'

'We'll make better time if we travel underwater,' Georgia said.

'But we must proceed with caution,' Borys said, tapping the compasses on the table. 'The ice floats on the surface but we could easily collide with the body of an iceberg that lies beneath the surface.'

Frost formed on the glass of the portholes, hardening into ice so that the view outside blurred and glazed. Sharp crackling sounds snapped through the hull of the sub.

'We had better submerge,' Borys murmured. 'The *Nautilus* is freezing. The extremes of temperature may crack her portholes or if any leftover water in the hull freezes it may burst the planks.'

Dakkar hurried up to the captain's seat and opened the ballast tanks. Slowly the *Nautilus* began to sink. More bumps and bangs resounded through the craft. Dakkar could just make out ice cracking from around the hull as they submerged.

Another few minutes and we might have been frozen in, he thought. The water bubbled around him and he gasped.

'It's so clear!' Georgia said, appearing beside him. 'And even in this cold, fish still swim!'

They stared out as the *Nautilus* went deeper, marvelling at the shoals of brown fish that swarmed along the bottom of the sea. Above them, the ice formed a ceiling of blue-white.

'Look!' Borys lamented down the speaking tube. 'So many fat fish and we can't catch any for our dinner!'

Dakkar allowed himself a smile, partly because the idea of Borys keeping lookout for icebergs through the portholes below reassured him.

'Why are we going so slowly?' Georgia said, frowning out into the water.

'Look over there,' Dakkar said, pointing to a distant white mass to the port side of the craft. 'If we strike something like that, we're done for.'

'Or like that,' Georgia said, pointing to another. 'Or that!'

Dakkar felt the blood drain from his face as more and more walls of ice loomed before them. Wherever he looked, icebergs blocked their way, leaving only narrow chasms between them.

'There are a lot of icebergs coming up,' Borys announced from below.

'Thanks – we'd noticed,' Dakkar said. 'It's too late to go under them. I'm going to have to steer between them. Hold on.'

He slowed the *Nautilus* right down, inching towards the sheet of ice that drifted before him. He licked his lips, breathing gently as he eased the wheel slightly to port. Georgia stood perfectly still beside him. The first berg went past silently and Dakkar pushed the sub to starboard as another, smaller mass of ice sailed by on the other side.

Sweat trickled down Dakkar's back. One wrong move and the massive chunks of ice would crush the *Nautilus* as if she were made of glass.

'Another one coming,' Borys said, sounding breathless down the speaking tube.

Dakkar swallowed hard and steered around a pointed fang of ice that jabbed down from the surface. Something scraped against the hull, stopping his breath for a second, then they slipped away from the obstacle.

More chunks of blue-white ice poked downward, forcing Dakkar to weave in and out of inverted crevasses and even tilt the *Nautilus* to avoid outcrops that might scupper them.

Gradually, they became less dense and Dakkar could relax slightly, slipping around a few larger, isolated icebergs.

'It looks safer now,' Borys replied. 'We should surface as soon as we can and head south-east for Guthaven.'

Guthaven turned out to be a small, huddled mixture of log cabins and stone buildings clinging to a black coast-line, blasted by the weather. The land rose behind the settlement, the white snow contrasting with the dark volcanic rock beneath. A wooden jetty completed a nat-ural quay, making it look like a protective arm crooked around the ships moored there. Through the gathering gloom of evening, Dakkar spied a couple of ships and some smaller vessels moored to the pier.

'There's a smaller wharf just along the shore,' Borys said. 'We'll moor there as it'll be more discreet. Best not to announce our arrival.'

Dakkar nodded. The appearance of a strange craft such as the *Nautilus* would raise many questions and news may get to Tomasz if they weren't careful.

He followed Borys's directions and took the *Nautilus* around a rocky headland. Soon they approached a line of smaller fish-ing boats that jostled each other along a short stone pier. A single hut stood on the coast like a guard on duty.

'We'll moor here,' Borys said. 'It's a short walk to Guthaven.'

'It doesn't look too pleasant out there,' Dakkar said, shivering a little despite the warmth of the submarine's cabin.

'Just as well we managed to stow some sensible cloth-ing,' Borys said, dragging a large sack up from the hatch below. He tipped out hooded coats and trousers made of some kind of hide.

'They stink,' Georgia said, wrinkling up her nose.

'Outside it's so cold that your skin can freeze to metal,' Borys said mildly. 'An exposed tip of the nose will become frostbitten and will rot off. The smell is a small price to pay for the defence against the freezing weather that these clothes afford.'

'Oh well,' Georgia grumbled, touching her freckled nose briefly and then grabbing one of the coats.

Soon they were all kitted out in thick leggings, hooded coats and mittens. Borys even gave them boots lined with fur.

Dakkar climbed down from the tower and promptly slipped over on the icy deck. He eased himself down the tower ladder and threw a line to a waiting fisherman who stood wide-eyed, staring at the *Nautilus*. He extended gloved hands to catch, his white eyes bulging in a brown weather-beaten face, and nearly dropped the rope in the water.

The cold gnawed at Dakkar despite his thick clothes but he shook himself and set about throwing another line.

Once the sub was moored, they climbed on to dry land. Borys dropped a gold coin into the fisherman's hand and said something in a strange language that was unfamiliar to Dakkar.

The fisherman held his hand away as if he were carrying a live scorpion and went back into the hut, shaking. He looked terrified.

'I told him that if I heard no rumours of our strange boat then he'd get another gold coin on our return,' Borys said. 'But if news got out about us then I'd be coming back to find him for a different reason.'

'Charming,' Dakkar muttered. 'Old habits die hard, I suppose.'

'We'll make our way to Larsen's Trading Post,' Borys said, ignoring the comment. His voice was muffled by the thick hood he wore. 'There's something of a tavern at the post and where there is drink, there is Tingenek.'

'He sounds very reliable,' Dakkar said as they trudged along the rough track towards Guthaven.

'He isn't,' Borys chuckled. 'And he's not to be trusted. But he is the best hunter in the land.'

They all fell silent. Dakkar listened to the crunch of their feet on the icy ground, wondering why he was heading out to meet a man he couldn't trust in a land he didn't know.

CHAPTER FIFTEEN
TINGENEK

Larsen's Trading Post stretched along the quay at Guthaven. A low, turf-roofed building with dark wooden walls, it looked chaotic and disorganised to Dakkar. Barrels and boxes cluttered the place and skins crowded against nets and ropes. Narrow-eyed men with round, weather-beaten faces smoked pipes and watched Dakkar and his friends as they walked into the courtyard at the front.

'Inuit hunters,' Borys whispered. 'They're the native people of this land. Clever and resourceful!' He gave one of these men a nod and went in, ducking under the low-hanging roof.

Inside the smell of unwashed bodies, oil lamps, uncured skins and fish assaulted Dakkar's senses. He grimaced and Borys laughed.

'This is no perfumed garden, my friend,' he said, patting Dakkar's shoulder. 'But you'd better get used to it!'

As Dakkar's eyes became accustomed to the gloom of the oil lamps, he made out a long counter that ran along one length of the room. At one end lay piles of fur pelts, barrels of pickled fish and stacks of planks and poles that Dakkar didn't recognise. At the other end a giant bear of a man with smouldering blue eyes, long tangled blond hair and a ragged beard leaned behind the counter, talking to an Inuit man who nursed a small glass. This end of the counter was more like a tavern, with kegs of beer and bottles of wine alongside tankards and beer stains.

'There are a lot of people in today,' Borys said in a low voice, scanning the other side of the room, where men filled the tables and chairs, drinking, playing cards and talking. Even here, the clutter of goods filled the gaps, creating little bays where men hid in the shadows.

'There were two ships moored at the quay,' Dakkar reminded him.

A pot-bellied stove stood in the centre of the tables, its chimney pipe running straight up to the roof; another warmed the furthest part of the room, which was lost in shadow.

'What do we do now?' Georgia said, casting her eyes all over the room. Some men met her gaze; others turned back to their drink and hid their faces.

'I'll have a word with Larsen,' Borys said, nodding to the giant behind the counter. 'He'll know where Tingenek is.'

Borys wandered over to the bar, where Larsen watched his approach suspiciously. Borys threw his hood back and the giant stopped polishing the tankard he was holding. He squinted hard over the counter.

'Borys?' he said. 'Is that you?'

'Of course it's me, Larsen,' Borys snorted. 'Who do you think it is? The Duke of Wellington?'

'Borys Oginski! My old friend!' Larsen bellowed, slapping his palms on the counter so hard that Dakkar fancied the whole building shook.

Borys looked alarmed and glanced around, pressing a finger to his lips. Larsen's face dropped and he too searched the room with worried eyes. Dakkar and Georgia hurried over to Borys.

'Keep your voice down,' Borys hissed. 'We need to keep our presence quiet!'

Larsen looked like a puppy that had disappointed his master. 'Borys, forgive me,' he said in a stage whisper. 'I did not realise! I thought you were that mad brother of yours.'

'Which one?' Borys said with a humourless chuckle.

Dakkar threw back his hood.

'And who do we have here?' Larsen roared, leaning over the counter and slapping Dakkar on the shoulder, sending him stumbling sideways into Georgia.

Borys gave Larsen a pained look. Larsen, realising his mistake, covered his mouth with his huge hands, his eyes wide.

'I am truly sorry, sir. Are you wanting to remain secret too?' the big man said through his fingers.

'This is …' Borys began, but Larsen held up a mighty hand, palm flat out.

'No. No. No. Don't tell me,' he said and gave a wink. 'That way, I don't know!'

'We're looking for Tingenek,' Borys said in a low voice that didn't hide his frustration.

'Tingenek?' Larsen folded his arms and stroked his beard as if he were solving some deep philosophical problem. Then his face brightened and he walked around to Dakkar's side of the counter. He turned to a barrel next to Dakkar. 'He's here!' Larsen beamed, tipping over the barrel.

A foul-smelling bundle of fur and beer bottles tumbled on to Dakkar's feet, making him leap back with a yelp. The bundle stirred and groaned and Dakkar realised it was a man, dressed like everyone in these parts. The man's face was screwed up as if a bright light shone in his face.

'Larsen, you ox brain,' the man grumbled. 'Why d'you wake me up?'

Larsen laughed. 'You have visitors, Tingenek.' Then his face grew serious and he leaned close to the man and whispered, 'It's Borys Oginski.'

Tingenek's eyes shot open and he gave out a long breath straight up at Dakkar, who covered his mouth and nose with the back of his hand. Tingenek leapt to his feet and fell down again immediately. He dragged himself up, leaning heavily on the counter. He stared at Borys as if he were a polar bear come to eat him.

'Borys,' he said, smiling a little too much. 'You look very well!'

'You look a mess,' Borys said, gripping Tingenek's shoulder and brushing him down with his other hand.

'The food here,' Tingenek spat. 'It's bad for my guts!' He let out a huge belch and turned to grin at Georgia, who gave a choking cry and turned away.

'You didn't turn down the fish soup I gave you last night,' Larsen said, pouting his lip in hurt disappointment.

'No, but it came up again!' Tingenek said, miming being sick.

'I think that's your fondness for beer, Tingenek,' Borys said with a fixed grin. 'I worry about your health.'

'The spirits will look after me,' Tingenek said. 'Now thank you, goodbye!' He tried to make a dash for the door but Borys still had hold of his shoulder and jerked him back.

'We need your help, Tingenek,' Borys said, his voice quiet and intimidating. Dakkar frowned and caught Georgia's eye.

'My help?' Tingenek moaned. 'Why would you need my help?'

'Let us sit,' Borys said, guiding Tingenek across the cluttered floor to a table in a corner. 'Larsen, bring lots of coffee and something to eat.'

'Something fishy?' Larsen said.

'Do you cook anything that isn't fishy?' Borys said.

'No,' Larsen admitted and shuffled away to the bar.

Borys sat Tingenek down next to him as Dakkar and Georgia dragged stools over to the table.

'The Heart of Vulcan, Tingenek. I've come to take it back,' Borys said in the same quiet voice. 'We need a guide ...'

Tingenek's face fell.

'Why do you need this man,' Dakkar said to Borys, 'if you know where the cave is?'

'Yeah, what's going on?' Georgia growled, half standing.

'I know where the cave is,' Borys said, grabbing Georgia's arm and easing her back to her seat. 'But the ice plain we have to cross is treacherous and only Tingenek can get us there safely. Right, Tingenek?'

'Why d'you steal it in the first place?' Tingenek said angrily. 'Tomasz has been stamping around like Nanuck with a fish hook in his rear.' He slumped on to the table, his head in his hands.

'Tomasz has been hunting you?' Dakkar tried to take in everything he was being told.

Tingenek nodded and heaved a huge sigh.

Larsen appeared at Georgia's shoulder with a tray of cups, a huge steaming coffee pot and a platter of fish and fresh bread. They all fell silent as Larsen placed the tray down then retreated to the counter. The smell made Dakkar's mouth water despite his shock.

'Of course he's been hunting Tingenek,' Borys said, lifting the coffee pot and pouring the contents into the cups. 'Tingenek helped me to hide the Heart.'

'And all the metal,' Tingenek said, his voice tinged with wonder. 'And rope and wheels ...'

'What does he mean?' Dakkar said, frowning.

'So you will guide us, Tingenek?' Borys said, ignoring Dakkar and stuffing a steaming mug of coffee into the Inuit's hand.

But before Tingenek could answer, a familiar voice said, 'Well, well, Prince Dakkar. Once again, I find you in dubious company ...'

Dakkar turned to see a man wrapped in skins and furs. A cruel, barbed hook poked from one sleeve of his coat and a scar ran down his pale cheek.

'Commander Blizzard!'

Borys leapt to his feet but Blizzard's men, who had been sitting at the tables surrounding them, stood first. Rifles and pistols appeared from nowhere, all pointed at Dakkar and his group.

CHAPTER SIXTEEN
CAPTURED

'Tie him up until I decide what to do with him,' Blizzard said, pointing at Borys.

Two marines, hulking and grim-faced, hurried forward and began binding ropes around Borys's wrists.

Dakkar watched as Tingenek, who had fallen down in the confusion, crawled across the floor on all fours, straight into the legs of a marine. Tingenek looked up, gave a simpering grin then crawled back to his chair, holding his wrists out for binding.

'I must protest, sir,' Borys began.

'You can protest all you want,' Blizzard said mildly. 'I'm not going to gag you. Now, Dakkar, suppose you tell me about these two and why you're here without Count Oginski?'

Something tightened in Dakkar's chest and rose into his throat. He wanted to scream out but he choked the emotion down. 'O-Oginski is ... dead,' he stammered and looked at Blizzard's feet.

Blizzard grabbed a chair and lowered himself on to it as he absorbed the news. 'Dead? How? When? You must tell me everything!'

Ignoring Borys's anguished face, Dakkar told him the whole story, pausing every now and then to swallow hard or catch his breath to avoid crying. Georgia took over for him sometimes when the details became too hard to relate.

When the tale was over, Blizzard spent a long while scratching the surface of the table with his hook.

'He was a great man,' he said at last. 'I'll miss him. He did our country a great service.' Blizzard stopped and fixed Dakkar with his steely blue eyes. 'He taught you well, Dakkar. You must be worthy of him ...'

'I will,' Dakkar said through gritted teeth.

The room fell quiet as they all thought on Oginski.

Finally, Borys broke the silence. 'So what brings the great Commander Blizzard to these frozen parts?' he said, as if he were conversing over the dining table and not bound hand and foot.

'The usual,' Blizzard said, matching Borys's tone. 'Reports of strange beasts attacking ships, of activity to the north, movement of men and ships, strange lights in the mountains. We tried to take HMS *Slaughter* round the north coast but there were too many icebergs – an unusual number, I'd say. All factors that point to the presence of one of the Oginski brothers! Or maybe two ...'

'I'm not the one you want,' Borys said. 'It's my brother Tomasz we must stop.'

'If you think for one minute that I would join forces with you then you're deluded,' Blizzard said coldly. 'Once I realised we couldn't get to the northern mountains by sea, I prepared for an expedition across the central ice of this barren land. We leave at first light. I would trust Dakkar and Georgia with my life. You, however, will remain under guard until I've decided what to do with you.'

'I think we should give him a chance, commander,' Dakkar said, glancing at Borys.

'If you had said you were *certain* we could trust him, Dakkar, I'd cut him free immediately,' Blizzard said with a faint smile. 'But you have a trace of doubt in your voice. No. He will remain here on HMS *Slaughter* with a small guard. We'll take the bulk of the marines and this man – Tingenek, is it? He can lead us to the Heart of Vulcan. From there we'll decide what to do.'

'Tomasz will find you and destroy you first,' Borys spat. 'Let me come with you – I can help!'

'Take him away,' Blizzard said to the marines guarding him.

Dakkar watched Borys being marched out of the room.

'Dakkar, Georgia, don't let them do this!' Borys pleaded as he passed them.

Dakkar pursed his lips and looked away.

The cries disappeared outside and Blizzard settled back into his chair. He raised his hooked hand.

'Do you approve?' He grinned.

'A flesh and blood hand would be better but, yes, it looks fearsome enough,' Dakkar said with a weak smile.

Earlier in the year Blizzard had lost his hand and lower arm to a dinosaur ridden by a Cryptos guard at the Battle of Waterloo.

'I'm surprised that you're serving again so quickly,' Georgia added.

'I can't say that I've fully recovered but these Oginski brothers don't wait for any man,' Blizzard muttered. 'I couldn't rest knowing they were still at large. Even while we were searching for him back in April, Marek Oginski completed his brother Kazmer's work and blew up Mount Tambora in the East Indies. Thousands of people died in the volcanic explosion and more perished in the tidal wave that followed. The next twelve months will see the sun blotted out by tons of volcanic ash. Famine will stalk the world, people will starve, there will be riots and revolutions in the major nations – just the right climate for Cryptos to flourish!'

'They never give up, do they? We foiled Kazmer's plan to blow up another volcano in the South Atlantic only last year,' Dakkar said. 'Stopping Tomasz is all the more urgent!'

'And so is rest!' Blizzard said. 'My men will assemble in a few hours. Until then, I suggest you try to get some sleep. We have two spare cabins on board HMS *Slaughter* – they're at your disposal.'

'Thank you, commander. I look forward to being on your ship again,' Dakkar said, watching as the marines led the Inuit hunter out of the tavern. 'I'd keep an eye on Tingenek. I don't think he's too keen on taking anyone to the Thermolith.'

'We'll keep him in the lap of luxury in the hold for now.' Blizzard laughed. 'Although I only trust his knowledge because your friend Borys sought him out.'

Blizzard led Dakkar and Georgia down the quay to where HMS *Slaughter* now rocked against the side, her three tall masts black against the darkening sky.

A marine saluted as they crossed the gangplank to the main deck. Most of the crew lay down below catching some sleep before the expedition began so the deck stood virtually empty but for a few guards.

'Get some rest now,' Blizzard said at the door of the spare cabin, which lay to the stern on the middle deck. He gave them a salute and disappeared into the gloom.

'I'll try, commander,' Dakkar muttered at the retreating figure, half crouching under the low ceiling.

'What're you up to, Dakkar?' Georgia whispered, eyeing him suspiciously.

'I want to talk to Borys,' Dakkar said, his voice hushed. 'Tingenek said something before Blizzard interrupted and I want to know what he meant.'

'But how can we find him?' Georgia said, looking around at the shadows that hid bales and boxes and barrels of supplies. 'We never ended up imprisoned on this ship.'

'No, but I was locked up on Blizzard's first ship – the one you sank, remember?' Dakkar said. Even in the semi-darkness, he could tell Georgia was blushing. 'I spent several weeks on that ship and I don't think the layout of this one will be much different.'

'I thought they'd kidnapped my Uncle Robert. There was no loss of life in that sinking,' Georgia muttered. 'Anyway, what do you want to know?'

'Tingenek mentioned metal and wheels,' Dakkar said. 'Why would Borys take so much equipment if he was only hiding the Heart of Vulcan in a hurry? It doesn't make sense.'

'That's a fair point,' Georgia said. 'I'm coming with you though.'

They crept through the mid deck. Row upon row of hammocks filled the space and they had to tiptoe past and creep under snoring sailors. More than once they brushed a dangling arm or foot, causing snorts and groans, but nobody woke.

The darkness on the lower deck thickened and the smell of the sea and stale urine made them grimace and splutter. A guard dozed in the corner, cradling a rifle on his lap. In the flickering light of an oil lamp, Dakkar saw a bundle of skins that huddled in the corner, snoring.

'Tingenek,' Georgia whispered.

'Quiet,' Dakkar replied. 'You'll –'

A flash of blinding light accompanied a roaring explosion that cut Dakkar's words dead. He was thrown back, smacking painfully into the side of the hold. Water gushed around his feet.

In the dim light, Dakkar saw the guard lying dead and Borys, waist deep in water, with spiny blue arms wrapped around his body and neck, dragging him down.

'Dakkar, help me,' he gasped as his head broke the surface.

Dakkar lunged forward but a spear thudded into the woodwork close to him. Borys gave a gargling scream and vanished beneath the water.

Gunshots mingled with the shouts of men on the upper decks. Georgia pulled herself to her feet. Dakkar tried to get to Borys again but water rushing into the ship sent her lurching sideways – and Dakkar with her. More Qalupalik emerged from beneath the deepening water, brandishing spears and sharp daggers.

'We're under attack,' Georgia said, gripping Dakkar's arm. 'And the ship is sinking!'

CHAPTER SEVENTEEN

FLAMES IN THE NIGHT

Freezing cold water swirled around Dakkar's thighs now and the Qalupalik hissed, spears poised.

'Why do they always seem to outnumber us?' Georgia said, quietly edging towards the steps that had brought them down there. 'Do you have a weapon?'

'This,' Dakkar said, wrenching the spear that had stuck in the plank next to him. It looked flimsy and useless in his fist but the sharp tip glimmered in the gloom. 'When I say, make a dash for the steps ...'

Sensing they had the advantage, the Qalupalik edged forward, jabbing their spears at Dakkar. Then the water between the Qalupalik and Dakkar erupted in a startling explosion of seawater and fur.

'Who woke me up?' Tingenek bellowed and swung his fist in a wide arc in front of him.

Fortunately Tingenek was facing the Qalupalik and three of them flew backward into the others. With a squeal of terror, the remaining creatures plunged under the water and into the darkness.

'Borys!' Dakkar shouted, jumping after them. But the water surged into the hold and he couldn't see a body anywhere.

'The Qalupalik took him,' Tingenek said. 'We must go up.' He pointed to the stairs.

Chaos gripped HMS *Slaughter*. Men scrambled to and fro as cries filled Dakkar's ears, mingling with the crackling of rifle fire from the upper decks. Oil lamps hanging from the low ceiling swung crazily as the ship listed to one side, making the deck a tilted obstacle course of loose rope and rolling barrels.

'Tomasz,' Georgia shouted. 'It's got to be!'

Another explosion rocked the ship, sending men stumbling into Dakkar. More gunfire spat up top as he rushed for the steps to the upper deck.

The heat of flames scorched Dakkar's cheeks as he popped his head out of the hatch on to the main deck. Burning sails flapped to the ground, igniting other canvas that lay stowed on deck. Fire had taken hold on the ship. All around him men shouted and hurried to the source of the fire with water buckets or tried to beat it with wet sheets of sail or tarpaulin. Men walked crablike against the tilt of the deck, sloshing valuable water as they went.

Other marines had formed ranks towards the stern of the ship and fired down on screeching Qalupalik, who hurled spears and small daggers.

'Didn't expect this kind of skulduggery,' Blizzard said, seeing Dakkar. The pale man raised his pistol and fired, sending a Qalupalik tumbling from the rigging. 'The blighters have wrecked my ship!'

'Borys has gone,' Dakkar panted. 'They've taken him.'

Another Qalupalik hurtled, screeching, across the uneven deck to hurl its spear, but a shot rang out. The Qalupalik fell, its blood pooling on the scrubbed planks.

'Commander!' A boy hurried past Dakkar, almost knocking him over. Blizzard had fallen and the boy helped him to his feet. A thin spear had pierced Blizzard's thigh. He cursed as he grabbed it and pulled it steadily out, leaning heavily on the boy.

'Well done, Fletcher,' Blizzard said, examining the cruel point. 'Good shooting, although you nearly took Prince Dakkar's ear off.'

'Sorry about that, mate,' Fletcher said, turning to grin at Dakkar. Fletcher looked about Dakkar's age, tanned by the salt and sun. His dirty mop of hair framed his mucky round face and almost hid his eyes.

'I am Prince Dakkar of Bundelkhand,' he murmured, eyeing Fletcher coldly. 'Not your mate.'

Gradually, the firing subsided as the Qalupalik fled, screeching into the night, plunging into the dark waters and vanishing with barely a ripple. Marines cursed and ran about, beating out the flames and tending to the wounded.

'Don't mind Dax,' Georgia said, giving him an annoying, playful punch. 'I'm Georgia Fulton.' She extended a hand to shake but the boy took her fingers and bowed, then kissed the back of her hand.

'The name's Fletcher, miss,' he said, giving a wink.

'I know,' Georgia said, reddening and snatching her hand away. 'Fletcher what?'

'Just Fletcher, miss,' he said with a second bow. 'Ship's boy.'

'Are we going to just stand around here exchanging pleasantries?' Dakkar said, scowling. 'Or are we going to get Commander Blizzard some medical attention?'

'Hmm, I do seem to be losing a lot of blood,' Blizzard said quite matter-of-factly. 'Doctor!'

A small man with spectacles and a bloody tunic came hurrying over. Blizzard sat on a barrel as the doctor cut away his trousers and poked at the wound.

Dakkar looked away yet the sight of the scorched ship wasn't much better. The marines had managed to quell the fire but many of the lines up to the burned sails hung charred and useless. The deck was blackened and many supplies had been lost.

'It'll take my men some time to repair this,' Blizzard muttered through gritted teeth.

A marine marched forward, pushing Tingenek before him. 'Found this fella trying to sneak off the ship, sir,' the marine said with a salute.

'I was just checking that the gangplank was secure,' Tingenek said, grinning.

'Good man, Baines,' Blizzard said, ignoring the Inuit and shifting uncomfortably as the doctor bandaged his leg.

'The Qalupalik have taken Borys,' Dakkar said quietly to Blizzard, 'so Tingenek is the only one left who knows where the Heart of Vulcan is hidden.'

'And if Tomasz has Borys then it's an even deadlier race against time,' Blizzard murmured. He fixed his eyes on the Inuit hunter. 'Tingenek, you're going to take us to the Thermolith by the quickest route possible.'

'Ha-ha,' Tingenek said, though he didn't sound amused. 'You're a really funny man. Why would I take you? It is certain death.' He waved an arm vaguely towards the dark shore. 'The Qalupalik own the ice out there!'

Blizzard raised his arm and brought the sharp hook close to Tingenek's cheek. 'Well, I'm here right now and I own this. Either you die on this deck or you take your chances out there with us. What's it to be?'

Tingenek licked his cracked lips and glanced from the side of the ship to Blizzard's hook as if calculating his chances of running. Then his face spilt into a fawning grin and he opened his arms.

'I see your point,' he said, forcing a laugh. 'I would be proud to lead you to the Heart of Vulcan!'

'Excellent choice,' Blizzard said, clapping him on the shoulder with his remaining hand. 'Baines, put some loose bindings on this man's hands and feet so he can't run away. We haven't a minute to waste.'

'But … but …' Tingenek stammered as Baines led him back down into the belly of the ship.

'Dakkar, you go with Fletcher here,' Blizzard said. 'He'll

show you which supplies we need to bring down to the quayside.'

'I'm sorry, commander, but you're not going anywhere,' the doctor said, polishing his glasses on his grubby shirt tails.

'I beg your pardon?' Blizzard said, blinking at the man.

'Stand up,' the doctor ordered.

Blizzard tried to get to his feet and gave a yell of pain, plunging forward. Dakkar caught him and eased him back on to the barrel.

'That spear did more damage than you think,' the doctor said. 'And you're still weak from losing that hand. You'd be a liability on the mission.'

'Well, you could have put it a little more delicately, doctor,' Blizzard said, swallowing down the pain and rubbing his leg. 'I do take your point, however.' He looked hard at Dakkar and then at Fletcher. 'Dakkar, I'm going to have to rethink my plan,' he said. 'I need men to repair the ship and men to guard her but I do want to find this Thermolith. I can give you an escort of ten men led by Baines – do you think that will be enough?'

'Georgia, Borys and I were going to find it with just Tingenek,' Dakkar said. 'Ten men will be more than enough.'

'Very well,' Blizzard said. 'I think Mr Fletcher would be keen to accompany you too. But be aware that my men will only escort you to and from this cave. They won't disobey orders and go off on some vengeance mission.'

'That's fine by me,' Dakkar said. 'We'll find the cave and bring back the Heart of Vulcan – that's all.'

'Good,' Blizzard said. He had begun to look paler, if that were possible, and Dakkar noticed a bead of sweat on his brow despite the cold. 'Fletcher will show you where the supplies are, assuming they're not all burned. Choose what you need and set off as soon as possible. There is no time to spare!' He hobbled off to organise the marines, to his doctor's despair.

'Come on, Dax,' Fletcher said with a sly smile. 'I'll show you the ropes!'

'Dax?' He stared at Georgia. 'This is your fault! My name is Dakkar!'

'My fault?' Georgia said, perplexed.

'Forgive me, your highness.' Fletcher smirked, bowing with a flourish. 'I'll watch my manners in future.'

Tingenek bustled forward, escorted by two of Blizzard's marines.

'This mission is foolish,' he said to Dakkar. 'Tomasz will send his Qalupalik and they will pick the meat off our frozen bones.'

'Maybe, maybe not,' Dakkar said. 'But we'll give him a good fight either way.'

'You don't understand,' Tingenek said, shaking his head. 'There are worse things than Qalupalik out on the ice. We're doomed.'

CHAPTER EIGHTEEN
THE ICE FIELD

The first feeble light of morning broke over the quayside.

'I hate the winter here,' Dakkar murmured to Georgia. 'The days are short and the nights are long.'

Commander Blizzard sat in a large wooden chair and stared at the depleted group of men before him. His pale face showed no emotion, although the scar that ran down one side of his cheek made him look as if he were frowning. Dakkar followed Blizzard's eyes as he surveyed the men wrapped in sealskins and armed to the teeth.

Tingenek busied himself around the sledges and the dogs that were to pull them. With Blizzard's permission, he had called on the help of some other local hunters. His two men were sombre and silent, their faces muffled under sealskin and scarves.

'This is Igaluk,' Tingenek said, pointing to the first

man. 'This is Onartok. Good hunters, good trackers. Not as good as me, of course!'

They gave a short bow to Blizzard and hurried off to lash the covers over the sledges and attach leather harnesses to the dogs.

'Those dogs look like wolves,' Georgia said, watching them warily. 'Why don't we get horses to pull the sleds?'

'The dogs are powerful and strong and used to the cold,' Fletcher said. 'Some of the officers kicked up a fuss when Commander Blizzard told us to use them but he just pointed to the Inuit and said, "If it's good enough for them, it's good enough for us." '

Dakkar looked at the sledges piled high with food and tents. 'They must be very strong,' he said, 'to pull all that.'

'I wish I was coming with you,' Blizzard said quietly. 'But HMS *Slaughter* must be protected and repaired.'

'We'll keep our rifles loaded and our wits about us,' Dakkar replied. 'Tomasz's creatures are still out there, waiting for us.'

'Good luck, Dakkar,' Blizzard said, giving him a salute. 'Sergeant Baines will command the men but will take advice from you.'

A burly marine in red uniform stood to attention at the mention of his name and gave Dakkar a nod. Dakkar recognised him as the man who had tied Tingenek up after the attack. Baines seemed to be bursting out of his jacket, his ruddy face hidden behind a thick copper beard.

Tingenek waved his readiness from the front of the group and Blizzard called the men to order. Soon the party left the ramshackle clutter of huts and sheds behind and trudged out into the frozen wastes of the ice field.

The dog sledges raced ahead, opening a huge gap between them and the marching soldiers, but Tingenek walked at Dakkar's side along with two guards.

'You think I'll go running off like a hare?' Tingenek grumbled, pulling a furious face. 'You don't trust me.'

'No, Tingenek, I don't,' Dakkar said.

Tingenek tapped his forehead. 'You're not stupid!' He smiled.

'The three hunters have a guard assigned to each of them, sir,' Sergeant Baines said. 'They'll set up camp as we agreed. Our tents will be ready when we arrive and food prepared.'

'You're too clever for me,' Tingenek said, giving a wide grin.

'I think Tingenek is smarter than he acts,' Georgia muttered to Dakkar. 'There's something about him I don't trust.'

'Well, he's all we've got,' Dakkar replied, 'now that Borys has been taken.'

They marched through a rolling landscape that reminded Dakkar of the moors around the castle. He swallowed hard, thinking of the last time he had seen it, blazing and broken. He coughed and blinked furiously, hoping that the men who walked alongside him didn't see.

'You all right, Dax?' Fletcher asked, genuine concern in his voice.

'It's Dakkar. And, yes, I'm fine.'

Gradually, as the day wore on, the rolling hills and coarse scrubby grass gave way to bare rock. They scrambled up piles of stone, silt filling their boots, but the white of the ice field glistened above them.

'Once we climb up here we are on the ice,' Tingenek said, beaming. 'Then fun begins!'

'Fun?' Dakkar said.

'Ice rivers,' Tingenek said, grinning even more. 'Crevasses, mountains!'

'It doesn't sound like fun,' Baines said, his eyes frosty. 'Bloomin' heathen land, if you ask me. One wrong move and the ice will be red with your blood.'

'I will keep us all safe,' the wily Inuit replied, narrowing his eyes. 'I love my own skin too!'

He hurried forward, followed by Baines, who had fixed his bayonet to his rifle. But Tingenek wasn't making a bid for freedom, just peering ahead.

'That much I do believe,' Dakkar muttered.

The land rose, rocks and gravel making climbing slippery and difficult. Finally Dakkar crested the hill and stared out, holding his breath in wonder.

The feeble daylight had almost died and Dakkar found himself staring out over a sea of ice. The wind-sculpted waves rippled on into the distance, where ice mountains and pillars pointed into the darkening sky. The ice seemed to glow pale and ghostly and, somewhere far off, a light flickered weakly.

'Our camp,' Tingenek said, appearing beside Dakkar and making him jump. 'We must get there soon.'

Georgia struggled up the bank and stood next to Dakkar, gazing at the ice plain in awe. Soon Fletcher and the marines all reached the top and stood to rest for a second.

'Tingenek,' Georgia said, 'is this the only way on to the ice plain?'

'The eagles fly on to the plain!' Tingenek said, licking his cracked lips. 'Unless you can fly, this one is best for us. Other ways take days more! Come along, come along. We must hurry!'

Walking became harder as they crunched over the ice. The ground felt slick and uneven under their feet, making them slip and stumble. Dakkar's thigh muscles burned. Conversation fell to a minimum as all eyes focused on the lights of the camp growing nearer. Dakkar grinned at the faint howling of the dogs.

'That's a sound I never thought I'd be pleased to hear,' he panted to Georgia.

Finally they could see the triangular tents made from sealskin stretched over long poles poked into the ice.

'Tupiq,' Tingenek said, pointing to the tents. 'They keep us safe from the cold.'

The sledges lay tied up with the dogs and a fire glowed inside each tent. The smell of a rich fishy broth made Dakkar's mouth water as he headed for the tents. Baines barked orders to the other marines and they began taking position as sentries or stowing their gear into the tupiqs.

Dakkar shivered at the delicious warmth that enveloped him as he ducked under the door flap of his tupiq and stepped in.

'This is a bit of all right!' Fletcher said, barging in and warming his hands at the portable iron stove that sat at the centre of the tent.

'Wrong tent, Fletcher,' Baines said as he entered. 'I think you'll find your bed is in the other one.'

'Oh, right, sir. Sorry, sir,' Fletcher said, fumbling a salute and hurrying outside.

Baines winked. 'He may be Blizzard's little darlin' but that don't mean I have to put up with him,' he said, listening to Fletcher arguing in the next tent with one of the marines about where his bed was. 'Cheeky blighter.'

'Like someone else I know,' Georgia giggled, staring at Dakkar.

'You're insulting a prince of the blood!' Dakkar said, but he half smiled.

Sleep didn't come easily. The ice floor made everything cold and, even though the hide beds they had brought lifted them off the ground, the air was deadly chill. Dakkar lay shivering, hugging himself, in his sealskin clothes. When he dozed, his dreams were a horrible mixture of the burning castle, Oginski falling and Borys being pulled into the depths.

Dakkar's eyes snapped open. A loud hiss had woken him up. Something was outside the tent – and it wanted to get in.

CHAPTER NINETEEN
NIGHT HUNTER

Dakkar lay frozen in his bed. The red glow of the stove lit the inside of the tent but gave little warmth. An occasional grunt or yawn drifted up from the hunched figures of the marines and Baines as they slept. Georgia lay in the bed nearest to him, her eyes wide open.

'Did you hear it too?' she whispered.

Dakkar nodded and eased himself up from the bed. The sound of something scraping across the ice made him frown. It was as if someone were dragging a large sack along the frozen ground just outside the tent.

The rifles lay propped against a rack by the door, loaded and ready to snatch up at the first sound of trouble. Dakkar inched over and closed his fingers round the barrel.

A muffled cry and the sound of boots stamping on snow outside made his stomach lurch. A single gunshot set the sledge dogs howling and sent marines spilling from their beds towards the rifle rack.

Baines jumped to his feet. 'Dakkar,' he called, 'what is it?'

'I don't know,' Dakkar replied.

Hurrying out of the tent into the freezing night, ignoring the yelp of the dogs, he ran around the back of the tent to where he had heard the hissing – and stopped dead.

The only evidence of the guard was a pool of blood on the ice and the man's rifle, broken in two. Dakkar turned his head away. There was no other sign of the attack apart from bloody smudges on the ice that trailed away into the darkness.

'Good Lord,' Baines gasped, joining Dakkar.

'It is the curse,' Tingenek whispered, appearing from the shadows of the tent. 'Tizheruk.'

'Tizheruk?' Dakkar said, shivering.

'His magic is great. Not even the sledge dogs hear him,' Tingenek said. 'He will take us one by one.'

'Not if I get a shot at him with this,' Baines muttered, lifting a wide-muzzled blunderbuss.

'Your guns cannot harm him. See.' Tingenek pointed to the shattered rifle on the ground. 'Look what he does to them.'

'What *is* Tizheruk?' Dakkar stared at the pool of blood and the gun.

Tingenek gave a dramatic shrug. 'If I knew that, I'd be dead! Maybe a demon made of ice, maybe a walrus with bear's teeth.'

'If it's that tough, how come it has to sneak up on us in the night?' Baines said loudly, noticing that more marines had gathered around the gory puddle. 'One good shot will see it off. Eh, lads?'

The marines murmured and nodded in agreement but there was little confidence in their faces.

'We'll double the guard,' Baines said briskly. 'Let's get ready to strike camp. I doubt anyone will sleep now. We'd better keep moving!'

The bustle of packing up seemed exaggerated to Dakkar, as if the men were eager to avoid thinking about what had just happened. Tupiqs were emptied and pulled down quickly and provisions lashed back on to the sledges. Soon they stood ready to leave, each man peering into the dark, the plume of their breath hiding their pale faces.

'It's horrible, thinking that thing is lurking out there, following us,' Georgia said to Dakkar as they began marching.

'Don't worry, ma'am,' Fletcher said gallantly. 'I'll protect you from the beast!'

'Thank you, kind sir,' Georgia said, suppressing a smirk. 'But I can look after myself quite well.'

'You haven't sailed with Commander Blizzard for long then, Fletcher?' Dakkar said, narrowing his eyes at the boy.

'No,' Fletcher said, not seeming to notice the coldness in Dakkar's voice. 'I was on the street when Blizzard found me and took me to the Naval Asylum. My dad died on a mission for Blizzard when I was a nipper and me mum turned to drink. I became a top-notch pickpocket and was quick on me heels too!'

'You stole from people?' Dakkar said. *So Blizzard employs criminals now?*

'Yeah, well.' Fletcher looked at the floor. 'Didn't have much choice. Either that or starve, I suppose.'

'I'm sorry,' Dakkar said, a pang of guilt washing over him. Not everyone had the advantages he'd had as a small child.

The thin line of men followed the dog sledges through the endless ridged waves of ice. The days dawned feebly and barely seemed to last. Dakkar's head swam as the world became a monotonous blur of white.

'Keep your wits about you, Dakkar,' Baines said, clapping him on the shoulder and making him start.

'Easy for him to say,' Georgia muttered. Baines seemed unaffected by cold or the hard, uneven ground that made every step an effort.

They snatched short hours of sleep, pitching one tupiq and cramming inside for warmth and security. The sound of shuffling boots crunching on the ice and that chilling hiss filled Dakkar's dreams.

Two guards vanished on the third night of their trek. They didn't even have a chance to fire a shot or warn anyone, and once more the dogs made no sound.

'Tizheruk again,' Tingenek said, looking grimly at the spot where the men had stood sentry.

'How could anything big enough to take two men move so quietly?' Fletcher said, shivering.

Dakkar swallowed hard. *Is this how it's going to end?* he thought. *Picked off one by one in the night?*

'I think we should try and outsmart it,' Dakkar said to Baines. 'This thing thinks it's got us where it wants us. What if we turn on it?'

Baines rubbed his beard and nodded. 'I like your spirit, Dakkar,' he said. 'The men are spoiling for a fight but we must reach this cave and find the Thermolith.'

'There won't be any of us left to do that. We're already down to seven marines,' Dakkar said, keeping his voice low. 'Tonight I suggest we pitch camp as usual then wait, armed and ready within the tents.'

Baines chewed the idea over, glancing at his men and back at Dakkar. 'Very well,' he said finally. 'We'll give it a go. We can't keep on losing men like this.'

That night, Dakkar suggested he, Georgia and Fletcher took a turn on guard. Baines was reluctant at first but Dakkar insisted.

'Just don't take any chances,' Baines said, eyeing Dakkar warily. 'First sign of trouble, let us know.'

Silence fell as Dakkar looked at Georgia and Fletcher. Their breath plumed in clouds, made silver by the moonlight. The moon illuminated everything but made the shadows deeper at the same time. A few yards from the tent, the dogs huddled, giving an occasional whine. Dakkar shivered.

'We should stand back to back –' Georgia suggested but a distant sound cut off her speech.

The sound of a heavy weight dragging or scraping across the ice. They all strained to listen. The dogs flattened their ears and crushed themselves to the ground as if trying to make themselves invisible.

'What *is* that thing?' Fletcher whispered. 'Even the dogs are terrified.'

'It's getting closer,' Dakkar said, scanning the darkness. 'But where from? Which direction?'

'It's over there,' Georgia whispered. She lifted her rifle and pointed towards the crest of a ridge.

'No, it's this way!' Fletcher said, hurrying away from the tent.

'Fletcher, no!'

Dakkar ran after him but Fletcher charged towards a distant island of rocks in the otherwise flat desert of ice before them.

CHAPTER TWENTY
BAD ICE

Fletcher stopped dead just ahead of Dakkar. The ice crunched under Dakkar's feet and the sound of his ragged breathing filled the air.

'Fletcher, you fool,' Dakkar snapped, catching his breath. 'What are you playing at?'

Fletcher squinted ahead into the darkness. 'I could've sworn I heard it,' he replied.

'We'd better get back to the camp,' Dakkar said. 'That thing could –'

A rifle cracked in the distance behind them and the howling from the sledge dogs began.

'Georgia!' Dakkar said, spinning on his heel and sprinting hard back towards the tent. Fletcher ran after him.

Georgia stood with the rifle trembling in her hands. Baines and the other marines stood around her, their weapons primed and ready, but there was no sign of any creature.

'Are you all right?' Dakkar said. 'Did you see anything?'

'Just a shape over there.' Georgia pointed to behind the tupiq. 'It moved so fast! Something large and white.'

'A polar bear, perhaps?' Baines said, unconvinced by his own suggestion.

Tingenek gave a snort. 'Tizheruk is clever. He won't be tricked by you.'

'Well, we scared it off for now,' Dakkar said. 'Georgia, Fletcher and I will keep guard for a while if you and your men want to go back to sleep.'

Baines nodded curtly.

The rest of the night passed uneventfully. Another day's weary march found the party standing at the edge of a smooth, blue patch of ice that stretched off into a haze. It seemed to glow like a summer sky frozen into the ground.

'This wasn't here before,' Tingenek muttered. 'A lake under thin ice. Not right.'

'You mean it's not natural?' Georgia said, frowning.

Tingenek shook his head. 'Not right,' he repeated. 'Not safe. We should go round.'

'But that would put days on to the journey,' Baines said, shielding his eyes and gazing across the expanse of blue ice. 'We can't afford to waste the time.'

'You're right,' Dakkar agreed. 'Tomasz has got Borys and they'll find the Heart of Vulcan while we just waste time.'

'I'm so glad I came,' Tingenek muttered, pulling a pained face. 'You ask me questions but don't listen to the answers. You're crazy!'

Tingenek said something to Igaluk and Onartok in Inuit. They shook their heads but resignedly drove the dogs on to the ice. Baines led the marines out on to the blue expanse.

Dakkar stepped on the glassy surface, half expecting it to shatter under his feet and plunge him into icy waters below. The ice held but gave an ominous, grating creak as he took each step.

'Will this ice hold us?' he asked Tingenek, who walked alongside him.

'It will hold me,' Tingenek murmured, his eyes fixed on Baines, who marched at the front of their line. 'He looks a bit fat. We should be fine.' Tingenek glanced down at his feet.

Dakkar followed his gaze. Water shifted under the clear ice. *Is there something down there, under the ice?*

A thin mist swirled around their feet as they walked gingerly across the frozen lake. The group bunched together, slipping often.

'We must be more than halfway now,' Dakkar panted, peering ahead. 'I think I can see the edge.'

'This is exhausting,' Georgia said. 'I skated on ice like this back at home.'

'I wish we had skates now,' Dakkar said, slithering along the ice. Something dark flashed beneath his feet, making him stumble and fall flat on his front.

'What was that?' Fletcher said, getting down to his knees and peering through the ice. More dark shapes flitted beneath their feet.

'Qalupalik!' Tingenek gasped.

The ice burst open ahead of Dakkar. The marine in front of him plunged into the icy blue water. He screamed as something pulled him down, then a hideous, spiny, blue creature leapt from the hole.

Dakkar lunged with the butt of his rifle, catching the Qalupalik square on the jaw. It squealed and fell to the ground. More holes appeared in the ice around the men as a horde of the Qalupalik grabbed at their legs.

Dakkar swung his rifle like a cricket bat, cracking the skull of any attacker who popped out of the ice. Georgia plunged her bayonet into the heart of a Qalupalik who tried to grab her. Thin cracks snaked between the ice holes accompanied by a splintering sound.

'They've weakened the ice,' Georgia gasped. 'It's breaking up!'

The noise grew louder, turning into a groan as the cracks widened and joined up. Dakkar began to back away as hairline cracks snaked towards him.

'Right, men,' Baines barked. 'Now's not the time for line formation. Break ranks and run for your bloomin' lives!'

'This way!' Tingenek yelled, leading them towards the edge of the ice.

Some marines clung to the sledges as they powered to safety. Others slipped, cursing the crumbling ice that snapped at their heels. Two weren't so lucky and were dragged screaming into the cruel waters.

The ice began to fragment into wobbling white islands of safety between freezing water and grasping blue hands.

The Qalupalik swam between the floes, leaping up and stabbing at the men with their spears. Their angry screams sounded thin and grating as they clawed and snapped at the soldiers.

Dakkar ran towards the solid ice, falling several times and whirling forward on his belly, arms splayed out, unable to slow down.

A marine stopped to help him. 'Keep going, sir.' He grinned as Dakkar clambered to his feet.

'Thank you –' Dakkar began, but his voice was drowned out by a loud crack as the ice at their feet collapsed.

The marine slid back, half in and half out of the water. Dakkar grabbed at his arms but dark forms slithered around the young man. Dakkar yelled in anguish as the Qalupalik wrapped their spiny arms around the marine's body and dragged him down into the freezing waters.

'Quickly!' Fletcher shouted, dragging Dakkar away.

Dakkar glanced back at the sea of bobbing ice floes. The rest of the troop was ahead of them now – he could see Georgia in the distance, her hood down and her long red hair flowing behind her. Ice broke with their every step, forcing them forward.

'Not far now,' Fletcher said, panting with the effort of leaping and staying upright on the vanishing ice.

Dakkar noticed that the others had stopped and were facing them now. They'd reached solid ground and Baines had arranged the remaining soldiers in volley formation. The angry screeching behind Dakkar told him why. He could imagine the swarm of enraged Qalupalik splashing through the water towards him and Fletcher, desperate to get one last victim.

Dakkar gave a yell and doubled his effort, leaping and scrabbling at the ice. It had broken in front of him and he found himself hopping from one wobbling island of ice to another.

Fletcher was ahead, bounding from floe to floe and making it look easy, but Dakkar could hear the boy's laboured breathing.

A Qalupalik burst out of the water in front of Dakkar only to explode in a cloud of blood as a bullet from the shore caught it. Three more icy rafts lay between him and the land. He cleared one but it started spinning and a Qalupalik leapt up on to his shoulder, trying to bite his ear off. Dakkar lashed out at it with his fist, sending it to the ground, where a bullet killed it.

Fletcher leapt and made it to the shore, lying on the ground, gasping for breath.

But Dakkar wasn't safe yet. The second ice island rocked close by. More gunfire told Dakkar that his pursuers were close. He threw himself on to the next island, landing painfully on his knees, his face close to the water.

The bulbous eyes of a Qalupalik loomed out of the gloom. Dakkar caught its stench of seawater and rotten fish, and jabbed his fingers into a slimy eye. With a squeal of rage the creature vanished.

Dakkar jumped to his feet, rolling, almost somersaulting, on to the last floe. It rocked upward with his weight and Dakkar felt himself sliding off towards the waiting water. And the equally eager Qalupalik.

CHAPTER TWENTY-ONE
DEATH STORM

Kicking his toes into the slick surface of the ice floe, Dakkar scrabbled forward, tipping the island back so that he no longer slipped down. But he could hear the gibbering and chattering of the Qalupalik behind him. A clawed hand grazed his foot and something snagged his trousers as he scrambled to his feet.

With one final effort, Dakkar mustered all his strength and leapt from the bobbing island, hurling himself at the shore. He had to keep low so that he was beneath the line of fire.

'Now!' Baines shouted.

The roar of every gun filled the air, peppering the water with shot and bringing scores of Qalupalik floating lifeless to the surface. The remaining attackers slipped back under the water and vanished, leaving Dakkar doubled up, panting for breath. The sound of gunfire still echoed as they all stared over the lake, now clouded with blood but giving no other sign of the comrades they'd lost.

Baines surveyed his remaining soldiers. 'Four left,' he muttered. 'Lost three good men then. Damn shame.' He shook himself. 'We'll get as far away from this cursed lake as possible then set up camp.'

They marched in glum silence for no more than an hour before Baines acknowledged that everyone was exhausted and needed rest.

Dakkar wondered at the coldness and hostility of the place. Before he arrived in England, he had only really seen snow on distant mountains. Now here he was, trudging through a frozen desert.

'The ground seems solid and safe here,' Dakkar said, stamping his foot on the ground.

The feeble sun stained the sky and ice alike with orange light so that Dakkar found it hard to say which was which.

Tingenek stood waiting for them, pulling a face. 'Not good sign,' he muttered, shadowing his eyes to stare at the rising sun. 'Storm is coming.'

'How can you tell?' Dakkar said.

'The sun,' he said, pointing to the pale disc in the hazy sky. 'Wrong colour. And the wind is growing.' He grinned. 'I can't smell the dogs when they fart.'

'What a lot of nonsense!' Fletcher snorted.

A gentle breeze picked up. Dakkar noticed small fragments of ice blowing free and catching on the fur hood of his jacket. A few bits stung his eyes, making him blink.

'I wouldn't dismiss it so readily, Fletcher,' Baines said, raising an eyebrow. 'Tingenek has lived in this freezing waste all his life. What do you reckon, Tingenek?'

'We make camp quick,' he said.

'You heard the man,' Baines shouted back across the men. 'Get a tent up at the double! And make sure everything is tied down as tight as possible.'

The wind grew stronger, whipping up larger ice fragments and sending them rattling against their coats and hoods. The tupiq flapped awkwardly, causing the men to wrestle with it.

Dakkar rushed over to help with the poles which, attached to the skins of the tent, seemed to have a life of their own, one striking him in the temple.

Ice filled the air now, hurled by the rising wind which moaned across the landscape, reducing the others to shadowy silhouettes. The tent wobbled and buckled. Dakkar could hear men cursing and hammering metal stakes into the ice but the metallic ringing was muted in the tumult.

'Hurry, men! Get that shelter up!' Baines shouted.

Pulling his hood hard over his face, Dakkar grabbed a guy rope, dragging it out and away from the tent alongside a struggling marine. Slowly, the tent went up, a triangular shadow shivering in the wintry onslaught.

Then Dakkar noticed another huge shape that was not the tent. Tall, like some kind of tower, it loomed above them all.

His heart thudded and his grip on the rope loosened, the wind snatching it from his hands. His workmate said something then looked up too. A sudden slackening in the gale parted the blinding flurry of ice particles and Dakkar held his breath.

An enormous snake, encased in slick white fur, swayed over them. Its flat head, covered in spines, bobbed on a muscular neck. Rows of sharp teeth filled the creature's long, grinning mouth and its gleaming red eyes bored into Dakkar's. The Tizheruk gave a massive hiss then lunged towards them.

Dakkar threw himself to one side, searching for the rifle he had put down to help with the tent. But ice covered everything, the wind burying items that lay still.

The marine beside him managed to fire a shot. The Tizheruk made no sound but lunged forward in a fluid motion, snatching up the marine and springing back into the thickening blizzard. Dakkar caught a confusing glimpse of matted white fur and scales; the briefest whiff of rotten meat was scoured from his senses by the sharp wind. But it was the cold, hate-filled eyes that stayed uppermost in his mind.

Shouts sprang up all around Dakkar and shadows staggered around in bewilderment. The Tizheruk vanished into the blizzard of ice with a hiss. A moment later, a gunshot rang out, followed by a scream torn away from Dakkar's hearing by the wind.

'Sergeant Baines!' Dakkar yelled. 'Georgia! Over here!'

He ran towards more cries and shots that sounded out in the storm.

Another shape appeared in front of him and Dakkar ran headlong into Fletcher. They both crashed to the ground, trying to untangle themselves from each other.

'It's you, Dax. Thank goodness!' Fletcher said, scrambling to his feet.

'Georgia!' Dakkar shouted, ignoring him.

The Tizheruk's hiss rose above the rising howl of the storm.

'Over here!' Georgia cried.

Tailed by Fletcher, Dakkar raced through the chaos, following her calls. Blood splattered the ice and Dakkar came across the body of another marine.

Georgia crouched, rifle at the ready. She leapt to her feet when Dakkar appeared. 'Thank the Lord you're safe!' she cried. 'I can't find Baines or the others.'

The shouts and hisses receded into the distance, to be replaced by the louder swishing of two sledges and the baying of dogs. Tingenek and his three men appeared on the sledges.

'Come quickly!' he said, waving them on.

Dakkar climbed on to Tingenek's sledge and helped Fletcher and Georgia on board. Some of the tents had been taken off so there was more room. Tingenek gave a shout and the dogs began to bark again, dragging the sledge through the chaos.

The wind's howling and the baying of the dogs blended into a deafening cacophony that left Dakkar confused about where they were going. They seemed to circle several times and then head in a straight line. Ice pelted by the wind made him screw his eyes tight shut and the rocking of the sledge disorientated him.

When Tingenek finally stopped, the wind still whipped

around them and darkness had begun to fall. The Inuit leapt off the sledge and searched the area. Then he, Igaluk and Onartok snatched shovels from the sledge and began to dig.

'What are you doing?' Dakkar yelled above the gale.

'We must make shelter or we die!' Tingenek bellowed.

'But what about Baines and the men?' Georgia cried, grabbing his arm.

Tingenek shook her off and carried on digging. 'Forget them!' he said savagely. 'They dead by now.'

'No!' Dakkar snapped. 'You don't know that. It can't be true!'

'We won't find them,' Tingenek growled. 'You want to die too? You stay out here, you freeze. You want to live? Then dig!'

Dakkar turned away, intending to grab the sledge and hurry back.

But back to where? he thought. *Which direction? And in this storm?*

Instead he grabbed a shovel off the sledge and began to dig alongside Tingenek. The Inuit was right. No man could survive in this storm. Not even Commander Blizzard's finest.

CHAPTER TWENTY-TWO
HUNTER OR PREY?

Dakkar sat in the ice hole, squashed side by side with Georgia, Fletcher, Tingenek, Igaluk and Onartok. Above their heads the storm raged, flinging ice across the entrance and harmonising with the howling of the dogs. Dakkar shivered.

The digging hadn't taken long and Dakkar was surprised at how quickly the Inuit fashioned an underground shelter from the ice. It amazed him how warm it was too, with the heat of the bodies packed into it.

'What about the dogs?' Fletcher asked.

'They're Greenland dogs!' Tingenek said with a broad grin. 'They love the cold.'

Dakkar felt helpless and miserable. He tried not to think of Baines stumbling around out there, at the mercy of the elements and the Tizheruk. *What chance does the poor man have? First Oginski, now Baines and his men. How many more must die before this madness is stopped?*

'We are safe here,' Tingenek said, his voice sounding strange and hollow in the ice shelter. 'We'll wait until the storm dies.'

'Then we look for the others,' Fletcher said wearily.

'If you want to waste time,' Tingenek said, shrugging. 'Nothing can live in a storm like this. Nothing human.'

Georgia sat up a little and fixed the Inuit with her steely gaze. 'We can't abandon them.'

Dakkar frowned. 'We have to keep going,' he said although each word weighed him down. 'Commander Blizzard would expect the mission to continue. We can only hope that Baines and the others have found some kind of shelter.'

'But we *have* to find them,' Fletcher said, staring at Dakkar. 'We can't just leave them to die!'

'If Tomasz forces Borys to tell him where the Thermolith is then whole cities will fall. Men, women and children will perish,' Dakkar said. 'Or have you forgotten?'

Fletcher slumped back against the wall of the den. 'No, I haven't …'

'All Oginskis are mad dogs,' Tingenek said, a mournful look on his face. 'I wish I'd never met them. No wonder I drink!'

Dakkar looked at the Inuit hunter and felt a pang of pity. Somehow the man had become involved in a plot not of his making. He thought of all the men who fought for the various Counts Cryptos and all their victims.

'My Oginski was a true friend,' Dakkar murmured. '*He* wasn't mad.'

'*Never* trust an Oginski,' Tingenek muttered, his eyes closing. In a few seconds he sat snoring.

Dakkar's eyes felt leaden too. The hard marching and early start, coupled with the storm and the attack, had exhausted him. Soon the gentle snores of the men lulled him into a shallow sleep laced with dreams of warm beaches and sun.

Dakkar woke with a start, wondering where he was. The walls of the ice hole seemed to close around him and someone gripped his arm. He yelled and tried to leap forward.

'Steady, Dakkar. You were dreaming!' Georgia said, pushing him back.

Dakkar stared at her and then around the den. He slumped against the icy wall as he remembered. Fletcher sat at his other side, rubbing his eyes.

'Where are Tingenek and the others?' Dakkar said, glancing at the empty wall opposite them.

'Checking all's clear and hunting for some food,' Georgia said. 'I hope.'

'I hope so too,' Dakkar said, half standing in the ice hole. 'I suppose Tingenek could have left us for dead back at the camp if he'd wanted to.'

They climbed out of the hole and squinted at the bright sunlight reflected off the ice.

'At least the storm has stopped,' Dakkar said, stretching and searching the landscape for a suitably private place to go.

Soon Tingenek, Igaluk and Onartok arrived back with a brace of what looked like pheasants with white feathers. Dakkar watched as Tingenek cut and skinned the birds rather than plucking them. He chopped their meat into chunks, offering it to Dakkar with bloody fingers.

'I prefer my food cooked,' Dakkar said, wrinkling his nose.

'Suit yourself,' Tingenek said, popping the meat into his mouth. 'We have no fire. You get cold and hungry soon. Wish you had meat then.'

Dakkar paused for a moment and turned to look at Georgia. She was already chewing, a telltale smudge of blood at the corner of her mouth.

'Can't afford to be squeamish, Dax,' she said, raising an eyebrow.

'Very well,' Dakkar said, taking a chunk of meat. It tasted of iron and salty blood. He chewed, fighting the urge to spit the slimy lump into the ice, then swallowed it down.

'Good, yes?' Tingenek beamed and nodded. He said something to Igaluk and Onartok, who grinned and nodded. 'We'll make an Inuit of you one day!'

'It ain't so bad,' Fletcher said, wolfing down a sliver of red meat.

'It'll keep me alive, I suppose,' Dakkar replied, taking another piece. 'And we'll need all our strength to find the Heart of Vulcan.'

Georgia and Fletcher looked meaningfully at Dakkar.

'No,' Dakkar said. 'We must go on.'

'Your friends are gone,' Tingenek said darkly. 'Ice covers everything after storm. Tizheruk eats the rest.'

Dakkar shuddered and swallowed his last piece of bird. 'Then on with the mission,' he said. 'Are you still willing to take us to the Heart of Vulcan?'

'If I go back to Guthaven then Tomasz finds me.' Tingenek drew a finger across his throat. 'Or Blizzard finds me.' He repeated the action. 'Tingenek can't rest until Heart of Vulcan is away from here. You can make it safe?'

'We'll find someone who can,' Dakkar said, wondering who that someone might be. 'Or we'll dump it at the bottom of the deepest ocean, where nobody will find it.'

'Then we will get Heart,' the hunter said. 'And then Tingenek will have peace.'

As they were a smaller party and all perched on the two dog sleds, they travelled faster than when they moved with the column of marines on foot. The dogs bayed and yelped as they rushed across the ice field. Ice sprayed up from the sledge runners and stung Dakkar's face, forcing him to keep his hood closed tight with one hand. This made holding on to the sledge more difficult and sometimes Dakkar would find himself leaning out to the side, perilously close to flying off. At other times Tingenek slowed right down so that the wind-cut ridges in the ice didn't send them bouncing high into the air and crashing to pieces on the hard ground.

They skirted around a huge crevasse so deep and dark that Dakkar could not see the bottom.

'Deep,' Tingenek said, his eyes widening. 'Some say it never end. Just keeps on going down.'

'I'm sure glad we don't have to cross it,' Georgia said.

'You fall in,' Tingenek said, grinning, 'you fall for ever.'

The rattling of the sledge shook Dakkar to his bones and he found his grip on the frame of the sledge loosening. He would doze and then lurch into wakefulness, almost pitching forward on to the hard ice and under the runners. The mountains grew closer and closer as the light faded. They bumped up a snow ridge, almost leaving the ground as they reached its peak, and the world opened out around them. In the distance, a spike of ice poked from the landscape like a dagger stabbed into the heart of the ice field.

'Tingenek, look!' Dakkar shouted above the swish of the runners.

'That's the ice cave?' Georgia said, narrowing her eyes.

'In there.' Tingenek grinned. Then he lost his smile. 'Dangerous place. Cursed. I never liked it.'

'As long as there's no Tizheruk,' Fletcher said, glancing behind them. 'I don't want to see *that* again!'

They stayed silent until the icy outcrop loomed above them. Staring up at it made Dakkar dizzy. A giant shard of ice that rose from the ground at such an improbable angle he felt it might crash down at any moment.

'That is entrance.' Tingenek pointed to a square doorway carved into the side of the ice spike. 'Tread carefully. Borys did not leave Heart of Vulcan unprotected.'

'You mean he left men guarding it?' Fletcher said, craning his neck to see into the doorway.

Tingenek shook his head. 'Traps. Snares. I don't know.'

'But if Borys hid the Thermolith so hurriedly,' Georgia wondered aloud, 'how did he have time to build them?'

'We spent long time digging cave,' Tingenek said. 'Borys was not in hurry.'

'I don't understand,' Georgia said.

'Maybe if we look inside we'll understand more,' Dakkar said, taking a pistol from the sledge and loading it.

He stepped forward and peered in. The day was failing fast but the white walls and floor reflected what little light there was. The entrance opened on to a corridor with smooth walls of cut ice. Dakkar stifled a gasp.

Someone sat at the end of the passage.

Drawing his pistol, Dakkar crept towards the figure and circled round. Whoever it was hadn't seen him yet. He leapt in front of the man, levelling his pistol.

'Don't move,' he intended to say, but the words stuck in his throat as he stared into the startled eyes of Borys Oginski.

CHAPTER TWENTY-THREE
DEATH DOUBLE

Borys Oginski didn't move. Dakkar recognised the plump face and the well-kept moustache, but a fine layer of frost coated Borys's hair and his skin had the grey pallor of death. His lifeless eyes stared through Dakkar.

Georgia appeared at Dakkar's shoulder and gazed down at the body. Dakkar reached out and gingerly tapped the dead man's cheek.

'He's frozen solid,' Dakkar said. 'It looks like he's been dead for a while.'

Dakkar noticed a leaf of paper folded in the body's fingers. Crouching down, he eased it from the stiff grasp and stood up again. It was a note written in fine, spidery letters.

'But how is that possible?' Georgia stammered. 'We saw Borys taken from the ship. He was dragged away by the Qalupalik just a few days ago ...'

'You saw what I wanted you to see,' said a voice behind them.

Dakkar stuffed the note into his jacket and turned.

A man the double of Borys in every way stood holding a pistol to Fletcher's throat. He had Fletcher's arm twisted painfully up his back.

'Sorry, Dakkar,' Fletcher said through gritted teeth. 'He took me by surprise. But there's a whole army of those horrible little fish-men up there – we didn't stand a chance.'

'Tomasz Oginski, I presume,' Dakkar said. 'And I take it you've been pretending to be Borys all along while your brother sat, frozen to death, in this cave.'

'What?' Georgia frowned, staring from the frozen body of Borys to the very-much-alive Tomasz.

'Your friend is correct, young lady,' Tomasz said. He looked over at the body of his twin. 'I need the Heart of Vulcan and he refused to give it to me.'

'But why can't you take it yourself?' Dakkar folded his arms. 'Let me guess. You haven't the wits to outsmart your brother's traps in this cave.'

'Borys was conspiring against me,' Tomasz growled. 'He found the Thermolith weeks before he told me about it. He built trap after trap to keep me away from it. I wouldn't be surprised if he was building this place long before he found the Heart of Vulcan. Do you realise how close we are to our castle in the mountains? He could have sneaked down here at any time.'

'So Borys did want to start afresh and leave his old life behind,' Georgia said.

'And you stopped him.' Dakkar pointed an accusing finger at Tomasz.

'Ha!' Tomasz said. 'Maybe he did, or maybe he wanted the Thermolith for himself. I knew I couldn't risk running the gauntlet of the traps in this cave so I decided to make him do so. I left him here to either make this place safe or to starve and freeze. He could've broken through his own traps and waited for me with the Heart but he decided he'd rather die than let me get it.'

'So the whole elaborate charade of pretending to be your brother was to entice us across the ocean to do your dirty work,' Dakkar said, staring in horror at Tomasz. 'You sent your own men and creatures against yourself just to convince us to help you.'

'I may not be a great engineer,' Tomasz said, 'but I can scheme with the best of them. I knew that either you or Franciszek or Miss Fulton would fall for my redemption and forgiveness story. I knew one of you would make it this far. Now you can get the Heart of Vulcan for me.'

'But you could've been killed at any time,' Georgia said. 'The Qalupalik attack, the eel, the giant turtle …'

Tomasz gave a smile. 'My Qalupalik would never actually have harmed me,' he said. 'I must admit, the turtle was just meant to help us stock up on supplies. And I certainly didn't think it would turn on us, but that just made the whole game a little more interesting.'

'But why us?' Dakkar said. 'Surely you have enough men to exhaust the traps in this cave?'

'Even the most fanatical Cryptos guards might think twice after seeing their comrades die so needlessly,' Tomasz said. 'You underestimate your genius, Prince

Dakkar. You've outwitted and defeated two of my brothers. That is no mean feat. If anyone can unpick the riddles and dangers of these tunnels it's you.'

'So you engineered all of this just to draw us in?' Georgia said, still struggling to believe what she was hearing. 'Even getting the Qalupalik to take you from HMS *Slaughter*?'

'Indeed! Knowing that poor old Borys had been kidnapped would only add extra urgency to your quest. My men picked me up from HMS *Slaughter* in the *Nautilus*,' Tomasz said, grinning. 'Oh yes, it was a simple thing to hand over your precious submarine to my men once we'd left for Larsen's Tavern. I confess, I was a little surprised to see Commander Blizzard in Guthaven, but the improvised destruction at the harbour only helped strengthen your resolve to complete the mission.'

'And then of course you had the small difficulty of our armed escort to get around,' Dakkar said.

'My Tizheruk dealt with them admirably.' Tomasz grinned. 'Why bother with a full assault when my monster can pick men off one by one?'

Dakkar lunged forward but Tomasz jabbed the pistol hard into Fletcher's throat, making him cry out.

'Admit it, Dakkar.' Tomasz grinned. 'You've been outclassed. HMS *Slaughter* is wrecked, Blizzard wounded with a fraction of his crew left. Oginski is no more. I have the *Nautilus* and soon I'll have the Heart of Vulcan.'

'Where's the *Nautilus* now?' Dakkar said. His stomach felt leaden as he swallowed down his fury at the mention of Oginski.

'She's in my castle,' Tomasz said mildly. 'Ready and waiting for the day when I will use her to destroy the navies of the world. But enough idle chit-chat. I'll keep Mr Fletcher and Miss Fulton here while you make your way into the tunnels and begin dismantling the traps.'

'Never,' Dakkar growled.

'Then I'll feed these two to the Tizheruk,' Tomasz said, pushing the pistol into Fletcher's neck. 'Piece by piece. Now, what's it to be?'

'Very well,' Dakkar sighed. 'But I want Georgia to come with me. If Borys has set as many traps as you think then two heads will be better than one.'

'True.' Tomasz nodded, relaxing his grip on Fletcher. 'And if one of you dies, the other can carry on. It'll save time.'

Dakkar felt his gut twist with rage but he gritted his teeth. 'I *will* avenge Oginski, you know,' he said, making his voice steely calm. He stared deep into Tomasz's eyes until the man gave a contemptuous snort and looked away.

'I don't care what you think,' Tomasz said. 'Just get me the Thermolith or this one dies. And just in case you have any other plans, my Tizheruk and its handlers will be close behind.'

A deafening hiss filled the passage and then a huge reptilian head reared up behind Tomasz. Georgia gave a scream and Fletcher struggled in Tomasz's grip.

Tingenek stepped up behind Tomasz, flanked by Igaluk and Onartok.

'Don't worry.' Tingenek grinned. 'Tizheruk won't hurt anyone unless I say. He's my pet. I've had him since he was this big.' Tingenek held out his hands.

'You were controlling it all along,' Dakkar murmured. 'And to think I almost trusted you.'

'Never trust *anyone*,' Tingenek said. He turned to Onartok and said something in his own language. The two Inuit laughed. Tingenek's smile dropped suddenly. 'Let's go.'

Dakkar gave a sigh and began walking down the corridor. In some ways, it reminded him of the ice hole they had slept in – the walls were white and glassy, as if polished. They curved up to form the ceiling, making the whole passageway round.

'I'd guess Borys used a Mole Machine to dig these tunnels,' Dakkar said to Georgia. The Mole Machine had been developed by the first Count Cryptos they had met, Kazmer. It was a huge drilling machine that could cut through rock.

'It would make short work of the ice,' Georgia said, nodding.

'What're you muttering about?' Tingenek said, leaning over Dakkar's shoulder.

Dakkar pushed him back gently. 'We have to talk, Tingenek. We're getting acquainted with how the tunnel was made,' he said. 'And I wouldn't walk too close behind us. If we set off a trap, you'll be caught too.'

Tingenek frowned, looked to the ceiling, then to the walls, hopping back several paces until he bumped into

Onartok. The Tizheruk's hiss filled the tunnel and Dakkar turned away from its cruel stare.

'That thing gives me the shivers,' Georgia grumbled.

'I think it would like to eat us,' Dakkar murmured. 'And once Tomasz has the Heart of Vulcan, what's to stop it?'

'Then we've got to use these traps to our advantage,' Georgia said in a low voice as she scanned the tunnel. 'We must find the traps and spring them without getting killed.'

The tunnels twisted and wound round themselves in a confusing maze of white. Every intersection looked the same.

'Tingenek,' Dakkar said, 'carve a cross or an arrow in the wall at each junction or we'll never get out of here.'

'Full of bright ideas.' Tingenek grunted and stabbed a cruel-looking dagger into the hard wall, sending splinters of ice scattering across the floor.

One tunnel led them down a dead end, forcing them to turn around. This left Dakkar and Georgia at the rear of the group. Tingenek and his men watched them but there was nowhere to run anyway – the Tizheruk's huge body blocked the tunnel ahead even if they got past the men. Its muscles rippled under the matted white fur as it squeezed itself along the passage. Dakkar was glad he couldn't see its long face full of razor teeth and those cold eyes.

The next tunnel they took widened out into a cave big enough for them to stand in. The exit stood at the opposite end of the room but Dakkar grabbed Georgia's shoulder before she could step into it. Georgia froze, her foot hovering over the entrance.

'A trap?' she whispered.

'Possibly,' Dakkar murmured. 'Look at the floor.'

The floor was perfectly round and covered with a dusting of crystal ice, but underneath it something shifted and moved.

'The walls look different too,' Georgia said, running her fingers along the entrance into the room. 'They're made of glass!'

'Now why would you do that?' Dakkar said, stroking the wall.

'Why have you stopped?' Tingenek said, inching forward. 'You found a trap?'

'I think so,' Dakkar said, tapping a cautious foot on to the floor of the room.

Nothing happened other than Tingenek taking a hasty step back.

Dakkar knelt down and scraped the flat of his hands across the floor. The crystalline powder cleared to reveal a blurred shadow beneath the glass.

'It's water underneath a glass floor,' he said. 'And there's something else.'

'Sharks,' Tingenek said, peering over Dakkar's shoulder once more. 'Many sharks.'

'How do they survive in this small pit?' Georgia said, kneeling next to Dakkar.

Igaluk said something and Tingenek translated for him. 'Igaluk says there may be deep tunnels under here leading to the sea, but they'd have to be very deep to go under the ice.'

'I've been in deep tunnels before. Very deep,' Dakkar said, turning his attention to where the floor met the wall. 'Maybe he's got a point. But why build a glass floor in –'

Dakkar didn't finish his sentence. He was placing his weight on the edge of the floor as he leaned in to examine the edge of the room. The floor began to dip away from him and Dakkar plunged forward.

For a dizzying moment, he saw the floor fall away, revealing sloshing water below. At the same time a huge mouth surged upward and Dakkar toppled towards snapping rows of teeth.

CHAPTER TWENTY-FOUR
A LEAP OF FAITH

The world became a fury of splashing water and gnashing teeth. Dakkar's stomach lurched with terror and vertigo as he plunged towards the hungry shark in the pit below. Then a hand grabbed his collar and suddenly he was jerked upward. He fell back into Georgia's arms, panting for breath.

'Don't mention it,' Georgia said, grinning. 'Look – the floor must be on a central axle. It's a flat plate that spins when weight is put on it.'

Dakkar watched the disc of the floor rotate and slip neatly back into place, covering the thrashing shark beneath.

'How we going to get across?' Tingenek shook his head. 'If we step on it that shark will get us.'

'What if we wedged the floor with knives or something?' Georgia said, squatting at the doorway and tapping the floor.

'We could try but that would work better if this side of the floor went upward, which it won't,' Dakkar said, stroking his chin. 'The fact that it's made of glass means it won't wedge as easily.'

'Yeah,' Georgia sighed. 'If the floor were made of ice the knives would dig into it, I guess.'

'Or we could have stabbed knives into the wall,' Dakkar said. 'But not with glass. It would just shatter or splinter.'

'You can't figure it out then?' Tingenek said, an evil grin spreading across his face. The Tizheruk hissed behind him.

'I didn't say that,' Dakkar muttered. 'It's going to take a leap of faith, that's all.'

'A leap of faith?' Tingenek looked dubious.

'Just get me some rope and some metal spikes,' Dakkar said. 'There should be some on the sledge.'

Onartok vanished back up the tunnel for the spikes and rope while Tingenek argued with Dakkar.

'If someone jumps to the centre of the disc, it won't tip down so quickly,' Georgia explained to Tingenek. 'Then they have to tip the far side of the disc and get to the other side before they fall.'

Tingenek frowned and shook his head. It took some time before he understood their plan.

'You think I let Dakkar jump over that hole and leave us behind?' he said, holding his hands up. 'You think I'm a crazy man?'

'If you think you can leap over to the centre of the disc before it tips up completely, then you can do it,' Dakkar said, shrugging. 'I'm probably the fastest and lightest –'

'*I* am, actually,' Georgia cut in. 'I'll do it.'

'Georgia, it's –' Dakkar began.

'Too dangerous?' Georgia raised an eyebrow at Dakkar. 'You know I can do this. Let me try.'

'The girl can go.' Tingenek nodded and slapped Dakkar in the chest. 'You stay with me.'

Finally, Onartok returned with the rope and spikes.

'So you know what to do,' Dakkar said, tying the rope around Georgia's waist. 'You'll have to move quickly to the top of the disc and see if you can tip it back before you fall off.'

'And if I do fall off?' Georgia said, looking pale.

'We'll drag you back up with this rope.' Dakkar gave a tight smile. 'But don't worry – you'll be fine!'

Georgia backed down the tunnel, pushing Tingenek aside and trying to ignore the hissing Tizheruk.

'Here we go!' she yelled, sprinting down the tunnel towards the entrance to the room.

With a grunt, she launched herself across the floor, landing just short of its centre. Dakkar could barely watch as the disc began to tilt down but Georgia scrabbled her feet on the floor and leapt forward again so that the disc began to return to a horizontal position.

'Keep going, Georgia!' Dakkar yelled.

The disc would begin to tilt downward again as Georgia ran for the far door. He held his breath, watching as she neared the door and the floor began to sink.

'Jump!' he shouted.

Georgia threw herself towards the exit as the ground beneath her sank and the water sloshed up over the edge. With a groan she hit the tunnel floor on the other side.

Dakkar hissed with relief.

'Now make the rope safe!' Tingenek shouted across.

'Thanks for your concern,' Georgia grumbled as she dragged herself to her feet.

She pulled one of the metal spikes and a mallet out of the small pouch slung around her shoulder. The sound of metal ringing on metal echoed in the tunnels as Dakkar watched her hammer the spike into the ice some distance into the far tunnel. She crouched over the spike, fumbling with the rope, then stood up with the rest of it coiled in her hand.

'You think you can catch this?' she said, taunting Tingenek with a few false swings of the rope. Then she let it fly across the cave without warning.

Tingenek flailed his arms out to catch it but the coils smacked him in the face.

Dakkar felt a gun barrel pressed against his neck.

Igaluk stared at him. 'No wrong move,' he said.

Dakkar shrugged. He picked up another metal spike and began driving it into the ground on their side.

'How we going to get across?' Tingenek snorted. 'Walk on the rope?'

'No,' Dakkar said, not pausing in his mallet blows. 'We're going to tie the rope hard against the ground. It'll stretch over the floor and stop the disc from flipping over.' He looked up and stared Tingenek in the eye. 'I hope.'

He tied the other end of the rope securely, stood up and threw the remaining length across to Georgia, who tied it again on her side. Soon there were three lengths of rope stretched across the cave floor.

Dakkar stepped on to the disc and watched as the other end rose up. The rope creaked as it went taut but it held as the disc pressed against it. He took another step but Tingenek barged past him, making the rope stretch and groan ominously.

'You go after Igaluk but before Onartok,' Tingenek said, striding across the room without looking down at the vibrating rope. He gave a little skip as he leapt into the doorway and next to Georgia.

Igaluk shambled over after Tingenek without seeming concerned – he even gave the rope a little tap with his foot.

'You need to be careful,' Dakkar called over to him. The sharp glass edges of the disc were gradually sawing at the fibres of the rope as it vibrated to and fro.

'No. *You* need to be careful.' Onartok laughed, giving Dakkar a shove to the floor.

The disc shivered as Dakkar inched across it. He could see loose strands of rope poking out from the main braid that held the floor level. Beneath him the dark shapes of the sharks swirled and circled in the water. Taking a breath, he half ran, half jumped across, Georgia grabbing him as he reached the threshold of the door.

Onartok stood at the other entrance, completely dwarfed by the Tizheruk that filled the tunnel behind him. The creature swayed its head, eyes still fixed on Dakkar, twitching its tail like an angry cat. Onartok stepped on to the floor and began walking slowly across. Igaluk called something that was obviously insulting and laughed. Onartok ignored him, watching his feet.

'Hurry!' Georgia cried as more of the rope twanged and unwound.

Onartok took three rapid steps then the rope gave a vicious snap and flew up into the air. The disc slid up behind Onartok, sending him slithering down into the hole. His scream ended abruptly as he hit the bubbling water. Then the floor closed over him.

Dakkar leapt forward but Tingenek grabbed his arm and pulled him back.

Onartok broke the surface once, thumping on the glass that sealed his escape, gave a muffled cry and then vanished again in a cloud of crimson blood.

The Tizheruk had been held back long enough. Onartok's death and the scent of blood pushed the creature into a frenzy. It coiled forward across the room towards Dakkar.

CHAPTER TWENTY-FIVE
DEATH COUNT

'Tingenek, stop that thing!' Dakkar yelled, backing away from the charging serpent.

But it was clear that Tingenek had lost control. The Inuit shouted and waved his hands, but the Tizheruk rose up with a deafening hiss, ready to strike. The floor began to tilt under it. The Tizheruk swung its head to and fro in confusion and snapped at the air as it slithered down the inclining floor into the splashing water.

The floor closed over the thrashing serpent but it carried on thumping and smashing against the hard glass. The floor flew up once, exposing the Tizheruk with the brown body of a Greenland shark in its teeth. Then the disc slammed shut and stayed closed at a slight angle.

'It's snapped the axle,' Dakkar said, pointing to the crooked floor. 'That won't open again. You've lost your pet.'

Tingenek produced a pistol from within his coat and pulled back the hammer. 'Tomasz still outside with your friend, Dakkar,' he said. 'We carry on.' But his voice wavered and Dakkar thought he looked pale.

The tunnels twisted a little further until they came to another chamber similar to the last one. This time, however, a grid had been drawn on to the ground with a number in each box.

'I don't think it's another false floor,' Dakkar said. 'But what do these numbers mean?'

'Look up there.' Georgia pointed to the far side of the room above the opposite door. A small wooden sign hung there. 'It says something.'

> *It's forty in English*
> *but cinq in French*
> *and more*

'What can that mean?' Dakkar wondered. 'It seems familiar somehow.'

'Doesn't make sense,' Tingenek grumbled, poking his nose into the room but not stepping through the entrance.

'Maybe it's a code,' Georgia said. 'Perhaps each letter means something – maybe a number.'

'The numbers aren't in order,' Dakkar said, looking over the squares. 'But the highest number, one hundred, is by the other door there – look.'

They stood staring at the floor. Dakkar couldn't shake the feeling that he knew the answer. It flitted around the corners of his mind, just out of reach. Tingenek and Igaluk slumped against the wall in the tunnel, heaving the occasional sigh and then jumping up to pace back and forth.

'Have you worked it out yet?' Tingenek said at last.

'Maybe,' Dakkar said, not taking his eyes off the numbers. 'But it takes time. This room requires a little more brainpower ...'

'Brainpower.' Tingenek snorted and took a step into the room, planting his foot on the square with a number five carved into it. Nothing happened. 'See?' he said, taking another step on to a number eight.

The stone tile sank a little and a metallic clink echoed around the chamber. Tingenek looked back at Dakkar, wide-eyed.

'Don't move,' Dakkar said. He could hear cogs whirring behind the walls. He turned to Igaluk. 'Don't you move either ...'

Igaluk stared at him through dead eyes. A wicked spear had sprung from the wall and its tip protruded from the man's chest, keeping him standing. Blood spread through the furs he wore and dripped to the floor. Dakkar gave a yell and fell back into Georgia, almost knocking her into the room. For a moment they stared in horror at the dead man.

'Don't look any more,' Dakkar said eventually, pulling Georgia away and focusing on the wobbling Tingenek. 'Very ingenious. Each of those square tiles must set off a spike in the walls, killing the people waiting to cross.'

'That's horrible,' Georgia said.

'Except tile number five didn't set off a trap,' Dakkar said. '*Five* in French is *cinq*.'

'Right,' Georgia said, her voice strained and dry. 'Is this a good time for a language lesson?'

'Forty is the only number in English whose letters run alphabetically. The letters in the word *cinq* are in alphabetical order too,' Dakkar said. 'C precedes I, which precedes N, which precedes Q, see? The safe tiles have numbers whose letters are in alphabetical order when you spell them in French. We just have to figure out which ones they are.'

'Right,' Georgia said. 'I think I know what you mean but there are a hundred tiles out there!'

'I bet there aren't that many,' Dakkar said, peering out.

The sight of Igaluk behind Dakkar and Georgia made Tingenek nearly fall over. He wobbled, trying to keep his balance. 'Shall I jump back?' he said.

'No.' Dakkar pointed to the next tile a few feet ahead of him. 'Jump to that one – number ten, *dix* in French.'

'You better be right,' Tingenek said.

'I've a feeling we'll be more sorry than you if I'm wrong,' Dakkar muttered, eyeing the walls nervously.

Tingenek jumped and managed to land his fur boots on the number ten.

'How about eleven?' Georgia said, frowning.

'*Onze*. No,' Dakkar said. 'Number two is next – *deux*. Can you see it, Tingenek?'

Tingenek nodded. 'It miles away.' But he leapt and managed to scramble on to it.

'The last one is by the door,' Dakkar said. '*Cent*, a hundred. You should be safe then.'

Tingenek hopped to tile one hundred and then leapt into the exit, heaving a sigh of relief.

'Come on, Georgia. You next,' Dakkar said, pointing at the first tile. Georgia leapt on to it and then the next easily, with Dakkar following.

Tingenek waited for them, his pistol still drawn. 'We carry on.'

'You don't need the gun, Tingenek,' Dakkar sighed, pushing the barrel away. 'Tomasz has our friend out there. Right now we should work together.'

'Don't you realise there's a reason that Tomasz sent you down here?' Georgia said. 'You're expendable. He doesn't care if you live or die. You said yourself, "never trust an Oginski", didn't you?'

Tingenek nodded and looked sorry for himself. 'I worked for Borys first.' He shook his head. 'We carried so much. Mechanical things, cables, pulleys. Everything for traps. Then Borys sent me away. But Tomasz knew. He made me work for him.'

'You could have turned the Tizheruk on him,' Dakkar murmured. 'Like you did to Sergeant Baines and his men.'

'Oginskis are hard to kill,' Tingenek said, his voice rising with fear. 'You don't know. Tomasz has more control over Tizheruk than me. I tell you, all Oginskis are mad dogs.'

'I never felt compelled to do their dirty work,' Dakkar said, curling his lip and turning away.

'Sometimes you not know whose dirty work you're doing,' Tingenek muttered after him.

Two simple tripwires blocked their way a little further down the tunnel. Dakkar cut them carefully and watched two blades swing uselessly into the path ahead.

The light didn't dim, staying constant despite the absence of torches or lamps.

'Mirrors must reflect what little daylight there is through these,' Georgia suggested, pointing to the circular holes in the ceiling. 'Clever.'

'Borys went to a lot of trouble to build this place,' Dakkar said, frowning as they walked on. 'It doesn't make sense.'

'He wanted to protect the Thermolith,' Georgia said with a shrug. 'He seems to have done a good job.'

'But this is so elaborate,' Dakkar said. 'Why not just bury the Heart and then destroy it at a later date? It's almost as if …'

'As if what?' Georgia said, rolling her eyes.

'As if he wanted us to get it,' Dakkar said. He gave a little laugh at the idea.

Georgia sighed. 'Dakkar, you always have to look for a more complicated answer than the one that's staring you in the face. Borys had just about enough time to hide the Heart of Vulcan, so he protected it. Maybe he thought he'd tell you about it himself then come and get it? Who knows?'

'Another room.' Tingenek nodded to the doorway at the end of the tunnel.

The room had two exits apart from the one in which they stood. One led to a tunnel that stretched off into shadow. The other, next to it, opened on to another chamber, lit by a warm glow. A sign above this entrance declared:

ONLY ONE DOOR, LEFT.

'There it is,' Tingenek said, hurrying towards the doorway. 'That warmth. It is Thermolith!'

'Tingenek, wait!' Dakkar shouted. 'That door is on our right. The sign, it says ...'

Dakkar tried to drag Tingenek back but he was out of reach and stepping through the doorway. Something swept past the door, displacing the air and making a heavy whooshing sound. Tingenek gave a startled scream. He was smashed aside like a rag doll by something solid and weighty, then vanished from sight.

Georgia and Dakkar hurried forward to the edge of the door. The heavy object swept past again, making them flinch back. Dakkar glimpsed Tingenek's shattered body smashed against the far wall.

'It's a giant pendulum,' Georgia whispered, looking pale and shocked. 'Swinging back and forth across the door. He should have listened.'

'Borys counted on our weariness to let us down,' Dakkar said heavily. 'Seeing the glow of the Thermolith clouded Tingenek's judgement.'

'I wish I could say he got what he deserved,' Georgia said, 'but I don't feel like that. This whole place is horrible. If Borys wanted to turn his back on evil ways, why make such a wicked place?'

'I don't know,' Dakkar sighed. 'Maybe he thought he could fight evil with evil?'

'Who'd have thought a simple comma could make the difference between life or death?' Georgia said quietly.

They walked down the other tunnel in silence. It curved round and doubled back on itself then ran straight for what seemed like ages. All Dakkar could hear was their breathing and the echo of their fur boots slapping on the floor.

The tunnel opened out into a huge chamber. Dakkar and Georgia exhaled in unison as they took in the awesome sight.

The roof of the cavern stretched high above them, vanishing into shadow. A black lake filled the centre of the cavern and a warm, red light spilled from a small island at the heart of the lake. The glassy walls reflected the ruby glow, illuminating the water and the cavern, making it feel warmer than it actually was. In the far corner they could see the pendulum, like a giant's hammer swinging back and forth across the tiny entrance. Tingenek's body looked small and distant against the wall.

'The Heart of Vulcan must be on that island,' Dakkar said, dragging his eyes away from the pendulum.

They hurried across to the lake. A small, wooden raft big enough for three people lay at the water's edge.

'There's our way across to the island,' Dakkar said, giving the raft a tap with his foot.

'The water's warm!' Georgia said, dabbling her fingertips into the glassy water. Ripples pooled out and lapped on the distant island, echoing around the cavern.

'It might not be wise to put your hand in the water,' Dakkar said. 'This place could still be full of traps.'

'You're right,' she said, pulling her hand away quickly. 'How do we get across the water?'

A sudden splash ahead of them stopped Dakkar's answer in his throat. The black water boiled and frothed as white coils rose to the surface, then it exploded and a huge snout burst up into the air above them.

'The Tizheruk!' Georgia screamed as the huge, hissing serpent shot up out of the lake.

CHAPTER TWENTY-SIX
RAGE AND REVENGE

The Tizheruk stabbed its long head at Dakkar, who hopped back, windmilling his arms as he tried not to fall into the water. He grabbed a knife from his belt and slashed at the creature.

'How did it get here?' Georgia said, pulling her own blade from its scabbard. 'I thought it had fallen into the pit.'

'The pit and this lake must be connected!' Dakkar yelled.

The Tizheruk jabbed its long snout forward again and Dakkar managed to cut a line across its nose, making the creature hiss and pull back.

'It doesn't look pleased to see us, that's for sure!' Georgia said, stabbing with her own dagger.

The Tizheruk glided around them and swung towards Georgia, opening its mouth wide. At the same time a tail snaked over the edge of the lake and swept Dakkar off his feet. He fell with a thump on the icy floor.

The Tizheruk bit down at Georgia. With a scream, she rolled sideways as the Tizheruk's long snout and teeth grazed the ice where she had stood. Dakkar leapt forward but the Tizheruk's tail sent him reeling back. He watched in horror as it snapped at Georgia again and again, pushing her against a rocky outcrop. The creature gave a triumphant hiss and closed in on Georgia, who stood with her dagger trembling in her hand.

Georgia gave a yell of defiance and stabbed at the Tizheruk's snout. It pulled back slightly and then jabbed forward, knocking Georgia against the rock. She slid to the floor stunned.

Dakkar stood helplessly, his knife in his hand. Georgia was his friend. He couldn't let her die. He thought of Oginski falling from the castle, Baines and his men disappearing in the storm. He thought of Tingenek and his hunters slain mercilessly in the tunnels of this place and a cold fury built up inside him. His heart pounded and he gritted his teeth.

'I'm sick of this,' Dakkar growled. 'I'm sick of losing anyone I care about. I'm sick of being chased. I'm sick of things trying to eat me. I've had enough! Do you hear me?'

With a howl that would have put a polar bear to flight, Dakkar launched himself on to the coils of the serpent. He sank the blade deep into its furred body, pulling it out and stabbing again, using the knife to climb up the snake towards its head.

The snake gave a maddened hiss and writhed around,

trying to shake Dakkar off. Dakkar's knuckles whitened as he gripped the handle of the knife, slamming it back into the body of the snake, climbing closer.

Blood slicked the matted fur now and the snake tried to turn right round to meet Dakkar's attack but he stabbed the serpent in the eye. With an agonised squeal, the Tizheruk lurched round, sending Dakkar whirling across the cavern and crashing against the wall. The snake reared up and plunged down on top of him. Dakkar just had time to raise his knife and screw his eyes shut.

He felt the Tizheruk's teeth tearing at the thick skin of his coat as if it were paper. A putrid, wet warmth engulfed his head, shoulders and arms, and he felt a pressure around his chest as he was lifted up. He stabbed forward into soft tissue again and again. Hot liquid gushed over him, stinging his eyes, choking him. Dakkar felt weightless. He felt the ground disappear as he rose up in the snake's mouth.

Pain lanced through his ribs and shoulders as the snake tried to bite down, but suddenly Dakkar fell free, landing hard on the icy floor of the cavern.

Opening his eyes, he saw the Tizheruk above him, glassy eyed and swaying. Then it fell towards him. Summoning all his energy, Dakkar threw himself to one side, curling into a ball as the dead snake fell to the ground with a disgusting, wet thud.

For a moment, only the sloshing of the water could be heard as the serpent, still half in the water, twitched its tail once or twice, then lay still. Georgia appeared above him.

'Dakkar, are you all right?' she said, shaking his shoulders. 'Eew!' She let him drop back and he banged his head on the ground. Georgia put a hand to her mouth. 'Oh! Sorry, but you're covered in snake blood!'

'Ouch.' Dakkar groaned, dragging himself to his feet. He gave the dead Tizheruk a savage kick in the snout and shuffled to the edge of the lake. 'And don't mention it.'

'Mention what?' Georgia gave a tight smile.

'Me saving your life.' Dakkar grinned back. He dragged the raft up out of the water and inspected it more closely. 'This has runners on it too,' he said, wincing at the ache in his muscles. 'It's a sledge as well as a raft.'

'Do you think the water's safe?' Georgia said, staring at the black surface.

'Hard to say,' Dakkar murmured. 'But I'll bet the Tizheruk will have killed or frightened off whatever there was in the water to get here. It looks quite shallow so hopefully it's too shallow for sharks.'

They paddled the raft across the lake, pushing away the floating coils of the dead serpent that lay half out of the water. The heat became stifling as they paddled nearer to the island and Dakkar had to squint against the harsh red glow from its centre. A square stone sarcophagus sat at the heart of the glow.

'The Thermolith must be in there,' Georgia said, pulling off her fur jacket as they got closer. 'It's so hot. I can hardly bear it.'

The water grew shallower and the raft scraped along the side of the island. Two rails poked out of the shingle and Dakkar eased the raft towards them, gliding it into position between the two rails with a loud click.

'The rails lead up to that stone box,' Dakkar said. 'They must be for moving the Thermolith around.'

Dakkar could feel his eyebrows singeing and his skin burning as they approached the stone box. A brilliant orange and red light burned within. It was like looking into a furnace. The air they breathed burned their throats and lungs now that they were so close to the Heart of Vulcan. The fur inside Dakkar's jacket was soaked with sweat and a foul-smelling steam rose off it.

Maybe this is why Borys's protection is so easy to get around, he thought. *The Thermolith kills you on its own.*

'We need to cover the box,' Georgia said. 'We can't stand that heat for long.'

Dakkar pointed to a rectangle of stone that lay on the ground. 'That looks like a lid. Can you get one end of it?'

He grunted as they lifted the heavy lid between them. Sweat trickled down his neck and back. Georgia's face grew red as they heaved the slab up on to the edge of the box.

A grating sound of stone on stone filled the cavern as they slid the lid across the top of the box. It was like turning off an oil lamp. The cavern became dull and gloomy and the suffocating heat evaporated. Dakkar and Georgia slumped, panting, to the ground.

'I could … hardly … breathe,' Georgia panted.

Dakkar dragged himself to his feet. 'Help me get this on to the raft,' he said, equally breathless. 'Let's get it outside.'

They pushed the stone box and it slid easily along the rails, although the heat of the Thermolith scorched them even through the stone and their gloves.

'It moves so effortlessly,' Georgia said as it rolled on to the raft.

'It's on metal rollers,' Dakkar observed. He shook his head. 'All too easy.'

'Three men have died,' Georgia said, looking appalled at Dakkar.

'I know but we're still alive,' he said. 'If you'd designed these traps, wouldn't you have made them a bit deadlier?'

'I'm not wicked enough to think up traps like these,' Georgia said, looking disgusted. 'I wouldn't know.'

A distant boom above and a loud crack made them start. A huge shard of ice crashed into the lake. Water began to trickle down from the roof of the cave.

'The cavern is collapsing,' Georgia said. 'Is that tricky enough for you?'

CHAPTER TWENTY-SEVEN
THE COLLAPSING CAVE

'We must have tripped something when we moved the Thermolith,' Dakkar said, staring back at the space where the Heart of Vulcan had rested. 'Of course! Why destroy the Thermolith when you can use it to draw your enemy in and bury him with it?'

'Can we go now?' Georgia said, leaping on to the raft.

Dakkar followed her and pushed the raft away from the shore.

More shards of ice and rock tumbled from above, splashing into the lake and rocking the raft so that Dakkar feared the Thermolith might slide off into the water.

They bumped against land and pushed the Heart of Vulcan off the raft. It slid easily across the slick ice but the water cascading from above made them slip as they pushed it at breakneck speed towards the door.

'The pendulum door!' Dakkar yelled. 'It's a short cut. We won't have time to get out if we go the longer way!'

'But we'll be crushed!' Georgia replied above the constant rumbling around them.

'Not if we time it,' he said. 'We can watch the swinging from this side. It won't take us by surprise.'

They hurtled towards the pendulum doorway, the sledge gaining pace as the runners cut into the icy floor.

'This thing is developing a life of its own!' Georgia shouted.

She dug her heels into the ground and was almost pulled from the sledge. The ground hissed by in a blur of white.

'Try and slow it down,' Dakkar said from the other side of the sledge.

'I just did and nearly came off,' Georgia snapped back. 'That door is coming up pretty fast!'

Dakkar's heart thudded. The wall was dangerously close and the pendulum had reached its apex and begun its descent.

'Get ready to leap off if we have to,' Dakkar said, crouching low against the side of the stone box. 'It's going to be a close shave!'

Rock and ice chunks rained down on them, crashing into the floor and kicking up a mist of ice particles. The doorway became wider and wider as it drew close and Dakkar could see the huge steel hammer swinging down.

We've got to stop – we'll never make it!

Dakkar slammed his feet into the ground but the sledge, powered by the weight of the Thermolith, had a momentum of its own. He gave a yelp. The cave flipped over and he found himself clinging to the back of the sledge and being dragged along on his stomach. Meltwater and fragments of ice splattered up into his face and he was thankful for the thick fur jacket protecting his body.

The hammer fell and Georgia screamed. Dakkar sensed a huge weight passing overhead as the hammer swung over him and behind the sledge, forcing the very air aside. Then the doorway flashed by them and suddenly they were careering through the room and into the tunnel beyond.

The tunnel turned and they veered up the side of the wall as they flew round the corner. Gritting his teeth, Dakkar scrambled on to the back of the sledge. Desperate to regain control of it, he crouched behind the hot stone box and scraped his foot along the ice. Georgia leaned out and eased her foot on to the edge of the tunnel too.

'This whole cavern will collapse in on us if we don't get out soon!' Georgia said above the roar.

The white walls of the tunnel flashed by as they pushed the Heart of Vulcan out of the cave.

And what will we do when we get to the surface? Dakkar thought. He hadn't had time to think about that since entering the cave. *Will we just hand the Heart of Vulcan over to Tomasz? He still has Fletcher!*

Dakkar's lungs burned and his breath clouded in front of him despite the warmth of the Thermolith. The sledge felt heavier and his legs were weakening. More and more ice fell, wet and clinging, matting his hair and clogging his eyes.

'I can see daylight,' Georgia yelled.

She stumbled and Dakkar had to pull her to her feet. The main entrance to the cavern appeared before them. Georgia slipped and fell again. Dakkar glimpsed figures silhouetted by the light ahead and Borys's body at the side of the tunnel. He gave the sledge one final push towards the outside world and turned to grab Georgia. Then the roaring filled his ears as ice and rock and snow poured down, slamming him to the ground. He heard Georgia scream, then all went black.

Dakkar sat in a darkened room. Oginski watched him across the huge oak table while Borys sat at the far end. Other shadowy characters muttered and shifted in their seats around him. Dakkar glimpsed Kazmer and Stefan, all deathly pale, eyes red and bloodshot. A metal cup was passed from one to the other until it came to Oginski, who sipped it and offered it to Dakkar.

'It's poison,' Oginski said, his voice distant and echoing. 'It's a poisoned chalice, Dakkar.'

'Nonsense,' Borys said, chuckling cruelly. 'It's a Trojan Horse, a feint. But poor stupid Tomasz needed it on a plate.'

The room erupted with laughter. Wicked, uproarious laughter …

Dakkar woke with a start. Something wet and foul-smelling slithered across his eyes and nose, making him cough. A huge black nose and a pink tongue surrounded in fur filled his vision. Claws scraped around him. He groaned, looking up. The dogs were digging him out of the snow.

Tomasz! The Thermolith!

Dakkar sat bolt upright, only to find himself buried up to the waist in snow. He heaved and rolled out of the hole that the dogs had made with their paws. Georgia was in a similar position so he crawled over and dragged her out. The dogs jumped around them, barking noisily and wagging their tails.

'Where have Tomasz and the others gone?' she said, shaking the snow and ice from her jacket. 'Where's the Heart of Vulcan?'

'They must have taken the Heart and left us for dead,' Dakkar said. 'But they can't have got far. Tomasz said his castle was close by.'

'Fletcher is still with them,' Georgia said, scanning the ground. 'Look – sled tracks. We can follow them. We've got to go after them.'

One last sledge stood abandoned, harnesses by its side, a dumb monument to Tingenek and his men who had been so casually sacrificed by Tomasz. Dakkar picked up the harness and turned it over in his hands while Georgia gathered the dogs together. Soon they had them ready to pull the sledge.

'Shout something to the dogs,' Georgia said, climbing on to the sledge.

'Go!' Dakkar said, pointing ahead where the tracks led.

'They aren't going to go anywhere like that.' Georgia snorted. 'SHOUT something, like … HEE-YAH!'

The dogs gave a yap and started off, almost throwing Dakkar from his perch at the back of the sledge. As the sledge picked up speed, it began to bounce and skip. The remaining dogs hurried after them, barking.

'If we can keep the tracks in sight,' Dakkar shouted over the yelping of the dogs and the swish of the sledge, 'then we can get to Tomasz and the Heart of Vulcan.' His strange dream came back to him, haunting him. 'What does the phrase "a poisoned chalice" mean to you?'

'Something that's passed to you and you think it's a wonderful thing, but it turns out to be bad,' Georgia called. 'Why?'

'I don't know but I've got a bad feeling about the Thermolith,' Dakkar said. 'We could be heading into terrible danger.'

'You mean Tomasz isn't terrible enough for you?' Georgia said, raising her eyebrows.

'Tomasz could be the least of our worries,' Dakkar muttered as he guided the sledge along the tracks left behind in the snow.

CHAPTER TWENTY-EIGHT
THE ICE CASTLE

At first the rocking and shaking of the sledge alarmed Dakkar. It slewed sideways and he couldn't control it. But as they moved on, he grew accustomed to the bucks and kicks it gave across the ice and he felt confident enough to shout the dogs on to greater efforts. Fatigue pressed down on him but he couldn't afford to think about it.

The land became rockier. Stone outcrops broke through the ice and Dakkar had to be careful not to crash the sledge.

The mouth of a deep ravine yawned before them, vanishing into shadows as the steep sides rose up and swallowed the feeble light. It grew darker the further they went inside and the dogs' baying echoed off the high walls.

They rattled around a sharp bend and Dakkar forgot his weariness.

'Tomasz's residence,' Georgia gasped.

A huge wall of white glacial ice filled the ravine ahead of them, blocking it completely. It rose high into the dark sky, making them feel tiny and insignificant. Towers and windows had been carved into the ice. One central tower was higher than the others, its top spreading out into a strange fortified platform like some some kind of giant metallic hammer.

A huge, arched gateway opened into the face of the glacier like a gaping mouth eager to devour them. Narrow windows, only wide enough for a musket barrel, dotted the walls either side. The wooden gate hung open and swung slightly in the wind that whistled up the ravine.

'It looks deserted,' Dakkar said as they approached the gateway.

'It could be a trap,' Georgia whispered back.

Dakkar stopped the sledge and began to unhitch the dogs. 'I doubt it,' he murmured.

Georgia helped him collect provisions from the sledge. They found some backpacks, which they filled with things that might prove useful.

'Why leave the castle unguarded?' she said, swinging her pack on to her shoulder.

'Only one way to find out,' he said and jogged in under the arch.

'I'm not so sure,' Georgia said. She hesitated for a second, then pursed her lips and hurried after him.

The darkness inside the castle gates brought Dakkar to a halt. He listened as he stared into the thick, inky blackness. The only noise was some banging and clanking above them.

'Everyone's up there.' Georgia's whispers echoed in the shadowy doorway.

'We need light,' Dakkar said. 'Do we have any lamps or a tinderbox in our pack?'

'Would this do?' Georgia said, pulling a small oil lamp from her pack. 'It's full of whale oil but I don't know how long it'll last.'

The yellow light of the lamp bounced off the polished icy surfaces of the wall.

'It's beautiful,' Georgia gasped.

'It's cold,' Dakkar muttered. 'Georgia?'

He looked round to see Georgia standing with her hands up. Two armed guards stood in a side doorway. One pressed a rifle barrel to her cheek.

'Put your hands up,' the other guard said, pulling back the hammer on his rifle. 'And get inside quickly. Count Tomasz will want to talk to you.'

Dakkar stared stubbornly, meeting the gaze of the guard.

'Do as he says, Dakkar,' Georgia said quietly. 'It might just get us closer to the Thermolith.'

'Very well,' Dakkar spat, putting his hands in the air.

With the gun barrels at their backs, Dakkar and Georgia made their way up flight after flight of icy stairs. Then the ice gave way to metal and their footsteps clanged noisily.

'We must be in the top part of the castle,' Dakkar said. 'Why is it made of metal?'

'Quiet!' One of the guards shoved him.

They stumbled along a passage through the belly of the metal platform. The ground shook gently beneath them as if it were trying to break free from the rest of the castle.

'Tell Count Tomasz we have prisoners and that we're ready to move,' the guard shouted.

A man ran ahead while three others appeared beside Dakkar, all dressed in the black Cryptos uniform. He could see the emblem on the shoulder and chest, a snake twisted around a large C with a trident behind them.

Accompanied by the three guards, they climbed another metal staircase and emerged on the mid deck of the building.

'This must be the flat metal top of the tower we saw from down below,' Dakkar said quietly as he gazed in wonder at the scene.

The huge space bustled with men lashing down boxes and struggling with massive metal bars driven into the floor. Each bar had three handles poking out of its sides and the men pushed at these handles, turning them slowly around.

'What're they doing?' Georgia said, frowning.

'It's as if they're unscrewing huge bolts,' Dakkar said. 'Bolts that hold the metal floor on to the ice castle!'

They clambered up the steps to the deck above. The cold wind stung Dakkar's face and the whole deck lurched. Up here Cryptos guards rushed about too, lashing ropes and turning valves that dotted the railings along the side of the deck.

'This whole platform reminds me of a ship,' Dakkar said, glancing around. 'We came through the base which was confined and full of cabins and then the second layer was like the gun deck of a frigate.'

'A bit wider and squarer,' Georgia agreed, 'but yes.'

Dakkar looked at the buildings at the front and rear of the platform. The rear platform looked like a poop deck – and there Tomasz stood like a captain, holding a ship's wheel. A large cylindrical shape sat in the middle of the platform, lashed down and covered with tarpaulins.

'The *Nautilus*!' Dakkar said. 'She's here, Georgia!'

The guards dragged Dakkar and Georgia across to the foot of this platform, where a flight of steps at either side led up to it.

'We caught them below, your excellency,' the guard said, saluting.

'Prince Dakkar, Miss Fulton, your ability to survive astounds me,' Tomasz said, looking down at them. 'I thought you had surely died under all that ice and snow. I underestimated you.'

'As long as I have breath, I'll stop you,' Dakkar spat, taking a step forward.

'I admire your spirit, Dakkar, truly I do.' Tomasz laughed. 'And I'm grateful to you too. You delivered the Heart of Vulcan into my hands.'

'I don't want your admiration,' Dakkar said sullenly. 'Or your gratitude.'

Tomasz gave a contemptuous snort. 'Well, it saved the life of your friend Fletcher,' he said, turning away.

'Where is he?' Georgia snapped.

'He is safe for now,' Tomasz said with a brief smile. 'His attempts at flattery amused me. He bought himself some time, probably in the vain hope he could stop me. But there is nothing any of you can do to stop me. We're ready to go. Observe!'

The guard heaved back a sliding metal door in the wall of the platform before them. Dakkar screwed up his face as the heat hit him. The hissing of pipes and the clanking machinery filled his senses and he stared into the cavernous hall.

Steam engines pumped pistons back and forth, and objects whirled on top of them in a confusing mass. At the centre sat the Heart of Vulcan, cradled in a metal throne, glowing beneath a huge tank. Pipes snaked in all directions from the tank.

'Hot air is pumped from the tank along these pipes – and behold!' Tomasz turned and gestured outside.

All along the platform, a hundred silk spheres ballooned from the pipes that skirted its edge. They blossomed like rare flowers, white and delicate, held in place by thin steel cable.

'My brother Borys would have been proud of his invention if he'd had the good sense to stay loyal to me.'

Beneath them, metal grated against the hard ice. The whole platform lurched. Dakkar's stomach jumped and he realised that they no longer rested on top of the castle.

'We are airborne!' Tomasz said, holding up his hands in a theatrical gesture. 'The whole fortress is flying!'

'That's impossible!' Georgia said. 'The platform is too heavy. It's made of metal –'

'Aluminium, my dear Miss Fulton.' Tomasz grinned. 'A strong but light metal. With the many balloons heated by the Heart of Vulcan, I can fly a whole fortress across the world. I can attack ships and armies without being touched, reduce whole cities to ash and rubble at my leisure. I am invincible!'

The ground swayed beneath them as the platform lifted into the air. The guards cheered and ran to the sides to look over, causing the whole craft to tilt gently.

Realising his chance, Dakkar lunged past the nearest guard and sprinted into the engine room. The noise of the machines there deafened him.

'Stop him, you fools!' Tomasz bellowed.

Dakkar could see the Thermolith glowing angrily in its seat. Its heat scorched his face.

If I can rip out the tubes, lower the pressure …

A searing pain burned through his skull and lights flashed before his eyes as his face struck the hard, metal floor. He lay stunned for a second then tried to stand. His legs felt like rubber. A guard had sprung from nowhere and hit Dakkar with a rifle butt in the back of the head. Two guards scooped him up under his armpits and dragged him back to Tomasz.

Guards pinned Georgia to the deck of the platform. Judging by the rifle on the floor and one guard's bloody nose, she had tried to react too.

'Give up, Dakkar,' Tomasz said with a smile. Then he narrowed his eyes. 'It's too late.'

CHAPTER TWENTY-NINE
MISDIRECTION!

'I'll give up when I've made you pay for the deaths of Oginski, Borys and all those men out on the ice field,' Dakkar snarled, straining against the grip of the guards.

'That will never happen,' Tomasz said coldly. 'And if we're talking about revenge, perhaps I should settle a few scores for my brothers Kazmer and Stefan. I'll let you live until we reach London.'

Georgia stared in horror at Tomasz. 'London? You mean you're going to attack a defenceless city?'

'Of course, my dear girl,' Tomasz said. He grinned and rubbed his hands together. 'You can bear witness as I rain fire and shot down on the capital of one of the world's proudest nations. I'll destroy its dockyards and barracks, its slums and palaces. I'll leave it a smouldering ruin and everyone will acknowledge that Tomasz Oginski is the most powerful of all!'

'You're a monster!' Georgia yelled. She leapt forward but Tomasz swiped at her with the back of his hand, sending her reeling.

'A monster?' Tomasz laughed. 'No, my dear. I'm a practical man. London will be merely an example. Other nations will make bargains with me – they'll join me or perish. Imagine the world united under one banner – the banner of Oginski, the banner of Cryptos!'

'You're insane,' Dakkar snarled. 'We'll find a way to stop you.'

'Lock these two up,' Tomasz bellowed to the guards. 'Put them with the other boy. When we reach London, Prince Dakkar will witness my ultimate victory before perishing.'

Dakkar and Georgia were bustled off down below and taken to a side room. One guard unlocked the door and then pushed them inside.

A small pallet bed filled one corner but that was all. The metal walls and floor made the room seem even colder and more unwelcoming. Fletcher looked up from where he sat on the bed, his eyes widening.

He jumped up. 'You're alive!' He beamed, grabbing Georgia's hands. 'I thought … well, I thought the worst when the ice cave collapsed.'

'We're alive,' Georgia said, hugging Fletcher. Dakkar felt a strange sting of envy and shook himself.

'Tomasz let you live,' Dakkar said, not quite posing the question why.

'When the Heart of Vulcan came flying out of that avalanche of ice and snow, he forgot all about me,' Fletcher said, rubbing his neck. 'They loaded the thing on to their sledge smartish and then one of the guards remembered me. I gave old Tomasz a bit of blarney about wanting to see his great invention – what a great man he was – and he bought it!'

'I wouldn't be so sure of your silver tongue,' Georgia said. 'You only bought yourself a few hours.'

Dakkar paced up and down in the cell, stopping every now and then to grip the bars of the small window and peer out.

'We *have* to get out,' he said.

'We can't,' Georgia said, slumping on the pallet bed in the corner. 'The door is metal, the walls are metal. This whole room is metal. We couldn't break out even if we had weapons!'

'That's it then?' Fletcher said, squatting with his back to the door. 'We just give up and wait for Tomasz to come for us?'

'No,' Dakkar snapped. His head ached horribly. 'I can't think straight but I know there's something I've forgotten.' He rubbed his temples and his hand fell to his chest. A piece of paper scraped his skin and he rummaged in the folds of his jacket. 'Of course, the note!'

Georgia stared at Dakkar as if he were mad. 'What note?'

'When I found Borys's body, he was holding a note,' Dakkar explained, unfolding it. 'I stuffed it inside my jacket when Tomasz appeared. It's suffered from the damp and cold a little but I can still read some of it.'

My dear brother,

You gave me a choice of helping you or dying in this wasteland and I chose the latter ... I hid the Heart of Vulcan in the ice cave for a reason ... hope you never ... past the defences I have laid ... the path you have chosen leads to destruction. I hand to you the poisoned chalice. Rest assured I shall have the last laugh.

Borys

'What can that mean?' Georgia said, snatching the soggy paper from Dakkar. It broke into pieces and she dropped it in disgust.

'It was too easy,' Dakkar said. 'A poisoned chalice. That's what the Heart of Vulcan is!'

Fletcher shook his head. 'What are you talking about?'

'Borys *wanted* Tomasz to get the Thermolith,' Dakkar said. 'He wanted him to have it and to install it in this fortress.'

'Talk sense, Dakkar,' Georgia said. 'We nearly died getting the Heart of Vulcan. It was well protected.'

'Misdirection,' Dakkar said. 'Can't you see?'

'No!'

'Borys and Tomasz hated each other –' Oginski said that back at the castle. Borys wanted to get rid of his not-so-bright but evil brother, you see?' Dakkar said slowly. 'But he came to realise that he could never be free of him.'

'Why didn't he just kill him?' Fletcher said.

'Because Tomasz is wary of Borys and Oginskis are hard to kill,' Dakkar said. 'Borys had to think up a clever ploy to finish him off.'

'So Borys built a huge ice cave and hid the Heart of Vulcan in it?' Georgia looked blankly at Dakkar.

'No!' Dakkar said, shaking his hands in frustration. 'Yes, Borys helped build a huge flying fortress but he knew it would never fly. Tomasz should be suspicious. He should be asking himself, "Why is my evil twin building me a super weapon?"'

'But we're flying now,' Fletcher said, scratching his head. 'It flies …'

'Borys said he put the Thermolith in the ice cave for a reason,' Dakkar said.

'To keep it safe from Tomasz, of course,' Georgia said, shrugging.

'No. To keep it cool,' Dakkar said. 'Once it's out of the ice cave, it'll begin to heat up even more.'

'Oh my stars,' Georgia whispered. 'It'll get hotter and hotter until it melts through the floor of the fortress itself.'

'Sending it crashing to the ground,' Dakkar finished, folding his arms.

Fletcher heaved a frustrated sigh. 'But surely Tomasz would suspect Borys of something like this?'

'No, because when Borys hid the Heart of Vulcan,' Georgia said slowly, 'Tomasz became so involved with finding the Thermolith and getting it out of its little hiding place that he forgot not to trust Borys.'

'Misdirection,' Dakkar said. 'The Heart of Vulcan is the trap, not all the blades and weapons set to protect it!'

'And when the trap springs,' Fletcher said miserably, 'we'll be caught in it too.'

CHAPTER THIRTY
SKY WRECK

'We should tell Tomasz,' Georgia said. 'Reason with him.'

'Good luck with that,' Dakkar said, rolling his eyes. 'Do you honestly think he'd believe us? Even if he did, would his wounded pride let him admit it's true?'

'All we can do is wait for the moment and be prepared to get away,' Fletcher said. 'We have to have a plan.'

Georgia threw her hands up. 'How can we have a plan when we don't know exactly what's going to happen or when? And in case you hadn't noticed, we're locked in a cell.'

But Dakkar nodded. 'Fletcher's right,' he said. 'We know that the *Nautilus* is sitting on the deck. We know she has the capability of flight. The first sign of trouble, we break out of here and head for the sub.'

Georgia opened her mouth to say something but the whole room tilted and shook, sending them tumbling against the wall. Outside the guard screamed as he fell the length of the passageway. The floor righted itself and they got to their feet.

'Now's our chance,' Dakkar said, peering through the grille in the door. 'We've got to get out.'

'But we're still locked in,' Fletcher said. 'What's changed?'

'The guard's unconscious,' Dakkar said, hurrying to the bed. 'We can try to pick the lock.'

'With what?' Georgia said, frowning.

Dakkar lifted the bed up and smashed it on the ground. The wooden frame splintered, revealing the sharp points of nails.

'We could try these for a start,' he said, worming a nail out of the wood.

Dakkar stooped at the keyhole and began to work the nail into the lock. The whole room shuddered, telling them that things weren't going well in the engine room.

'I thought you'd be a dab hand at this kind of thing, Fletcher,' he said, wiggling the nail and pushing a second one in.

'What, me? A house-breaker? Nah!' Fletcher snorted, watching over Dakkar's shoulder. 'I was an honest-to-goodness pickpocket. I only took what I needed – wasn't greedy.'

'I'm glad to hear it,' Dakkar said, grinning at the metallic clunk from the lock. He stood up and pushed the door open.

Barrels and boxes lay scattered across the lower deck of the platform. Guards rushed backward and forward, trying to secure cannon and ammunition that had broken free. The platform shook again and tilted to port. Nobody even looked at Dakkar or the others as they raced along to the upper deck.

The wind whipped at their faces as they stepped up into the open air and Dakkar almost fell over as the fortress pitched again. The balloons rattled against each other in the gale. Dakkar noticed some had deflated. Men staggered from side to side on the platform, trying to stay on their feet as it rolled like a ship in a storm.

Dakkar turned to Georgia and Fletcher. 'Quickly,' he said. 'Find something to cut the ropes on the *Nautilus*.'

Fletcher hurried around the back of the sub. Dakkar and Georgia crept between bellowing men who tried to keep their balance on the foundering platform. Someone screamed and fell over the side.

An axe slid past Dakkar and he made to grab it but a foot ground painfully on to his fingers. Tomasz stood, glowering down at him.

'What have you done to the Thermolith?' he demanded, grabbing Dakkar by the throat. 'It's melting through its cradle, becoming hotter and hotter. What have you done? Tell me!'

Dakkar couldn't believe the man's strength. Tomasz's fingers closed like a noose around his neck, choking him. He grappled with the strong hands, trying to break free.

'It wasn't us!' Georgia shouted, running over and pulling at Tomasz's arm. 'It was Borys. He tricked you.' She beat at his shoulders. 'Borys knew the Thermolith would overheat. He knew it would do this.'

Dakkar couldn't breathe. His head felt as though it would explode. The world around him began to fade and go black. He felt weightless, then his breath rushed from his body and a stabbing pain shot up his back as he hit the ground.

Georgia had leapt on to Tomasz's back and was clawing at his face. Dakkar had been thrown aside.

Tomasz struck out, sending Georgia staggering. Dakkar leapt forward, jabbing at the count with his fist.

'Georgia, help Fletcher get the *Nautilus* ready,' Dakkar said. 'I'll deal with *this*.'

'But, Dakkar!' Georgia shouted.

'Go!' Dakkar yelled as the fortress whirled around, sending more men screaming to their deaths.

Georgia fell away, grabbing hold of crates and boxes for stability.

'The Heart of Vulcan is overheating! It's melting through the deck of the fortress,' Tomasz panted, circling the deck with his fists raised. 'We're doomed but I'll take you down with me.'

Dakkar lashed out with a punch but Tomasz, surprisingly fast for so portly a man, ducked and landed a fist on Dakkar's cheek. They fell back towards the engine room. Dakkar launched himself at Tomasz's ankles, tackling him to the ground, but Tomasz kicked out. The hours without sleep and the stresses of the previous few days weighed heavily on Dakkar. He fell back and Tomasz clambered to his feet.

At the centre of the fortress's deck, Fletcher struggled with the ropes that held the *Nautilus* down.

Tomasz climbed up the steps to the back of the platform and grabbed the huge ship's wheel, spinning it to the left. The whole fortress groaned as it turned, sending everyone staggering across the floor.

'If we're going to die then let's all go together, eh, Dakkar?' Tomasz cackled, his eyes wide.

Dakkar dragged himself up the steps. 'Tomasz, no!' he cried.

'Borys thought he could trick me, did he?' Tomasz growled. 'Well, I'll show him! I'll ditch this whole fortress into the sea. At least I'll have the satisfaction of knowing I've had revenge on you, Prince Dakkar.'

Dakkar staggered over to the cradle that had once held the Heart of Vulcan and stared down the gaping hole in the middle of the melted heap. He had to shield his eyes from the glare below as the rock scorched its way through metal.

'The Thermolith is no longer supplying hot air to the balloons!' Georgia yelled, pointing to the sagging silk bags that were becoming softer by the second.

She was on the *Nautilus* now. Fletcher had dragged the ropes and tarpaulins free but she was starting to slide across the deck.

'Georgia, Fletcher, get inside!' Dakkar yelled. 'Start the engines!'

The fortress whirled round faster, sending everyone stumbling. Even Tomasz lost his hold and fell, sliding across the slippery metal floor. Guards screamed as they hurtled towards the low pipework wall that edged the platform and tumbled over it.

Georgia slipped on the sub's tower ladder and almost fell. Fletcher ran to get on to the upper deck as the *Nautilus* slid towards the edge of the fortress.

Summoning all his strength, Dakkar crawled towards the ship's wheel, hauling himself up on to it. He pulled at it, trying to slow the mad whirl, so that Fletcher and Georgia could get into the submarine.

'What are you doing?' Tomasz roared, staggering across the platform towards him.

'Borys is the one who brought us all on to this death-trap,' Dakkar said, heaving at the wheel. He could see the steely grey of the sea below now. 'Wouldn't it be better to live and get revenge on those who *really* betrayed you?'

'My brother is dead.' Tomasz charged towards Dakkar. 'How can I get revenge on him?'

Dakkar braced himself for the attack, but before Tomasz could reach him the fortress shook and a huge explosion deafened them. Dakkar saw the Heart of Vulcan thrown high into the air, streaking like a comet, then it plummeted over the side and into the sea. Smoke billowed up from the lower decks of the platform. Some balloons broke their moorings, causing the fortress to sag to one side again. Men screamed and tumbled over the side.

'The ammunition has ignited in the storerooms below!' someone screamed as another explosion rocked them, sending fragments of hot metal pinging and buzzing around their heads.

'Borys even designed the fortress so that the gun-powder store lies directly under the engine room,' Dakkar muttered to himself.

The fortress tilted again and he slid straight towards Tomasz, who clung to the rails at the side of the platform, struggling to keep balance. He grinned as Dakkar slid nearer across the slick metal.

The *Nautilus* gave an ominous groan and slipped over the side. Dakkar couldn't see Georgia or Fletcher.

'My only consolation is that I'm going to kill you before we all go down,' Tomasz snarled, reaching out for him.

Dakkar kicked his legs out, trying to slow his fall, but Tomasz drew nearer. At the last moment, just as Dakkar was about to slide under Tomasz, he rolled and grabbed the man's leg, his momentum dragging Tomasz down.

Tomasz fell heavily and the two of them continued to slide. Dakkar glimpsed boxes, ropes, bodies of guards racing past him. Then he saw stars as Tomasz's fist struck him in the temple. All the while they slipped closer and closer to the edge of the falling fortress.

CHAPTER THIRTY-ONE
DEATH FALL

'This is for my brother Kazmer ...' Tomasz punched. 'And this is for Stefan ...' He raised his fist again but then vanished from view.

They had struck the railings at the perimeter of the fortress. Tomasz, being on top, fell backward over the edge. Dakkar slammed his feet against the pipes and stopped his fall. He dragged himself up, groaning.

A gloved hand gripped the edge of the wall. Dakkar looked over at Tomasz, who held on by his fingertips.

'Help me,' Tomasz gasped from below.

He tried to kill me, Dakkar thought. *He killed Oginski.*

Tomasz glared up at him, his fingers slipping from the edge.

'Are you going to let me die?' Tomasz said, sweat dripping from his brow. 'Then you're no better than I am.'

'Men can become so consumed by revenge that they become monsters,' Oginski had once said to him when he was younger.

'*Are you a monster?*' Oginski's voice echoed in his mind.

Dakkar lunged over the side and grabbed Tomasz's arm with both hands and tried to heave him up.

'Fool!' Tomasz spat and gripped Dakkar's jacket.

'Tomasz, no!' Dakkar yelled, but it was too late.

Once more he felt weightless as he and Tomasz plunged from the side of the fortress.

'Bad luck, Prince Dakkar,' Tomasz yelled over the wind that rushed through their ears. The sea waited for them below. 'In the end you lost!'

This is it, Dakkar thought. *I'm going to die.*

Something pale and round bobbed and fluttered beneath them. It was a balloon from the fortress that had lost hot air and gas. It drifted at a lower level but still had some buoyancy.

Dakkar twisted his head and sank his teeth into Tomasz's chubby arm. With a yell of surprise, he released Dakkar.

Kicking away from Tomasz and twisting his aching body, Dakkar saw that the balloon had floated directly below him. As the rippling silk came level with him, he spotted a cable that trailed beneath the canopy of the balloon and made a grab for it. The steel burned his palms even through his gloves, making him scream, but he gripped tightly. As the balloon slowed his fall, he felt as if his shoulder muscles would burst. Breath rushed from his lungs and he groaned as he swung from the cables.

He watched as Tomasz gradually vanished beneath him, looking up with an expression of wide-eyed disbelief.

Dakkar knew he should have felt triumphant. Oginski's

killer had been paid back. But Oginski was still dead and Dakkar felt empty.

Nausea pressed at Dakkar's throat and every muscle in his body pulsed but he hung on as the balloon slowly descended under his weight, bringing the sea nearer and nearer.

He looked up at the fortress, a massive square meteorite dragging a trail of smoke and flame across the cloudy skies. Chunks of metal, boxes, sacks and bodies all cascaded down into the waters as it fell.

Dakkar watched as the glowing Heart of Vulcan seared a path through the cold air and into the freezing waters, its extreme heat reacting violently with the icy sea. It was gone.

And the *Nautilus* was nowhere to be seen.

'Georgia!' Dakkar whispered.

Tears pricked his eyes as the fortress crashed into the sea, throwing up a huge wave of water. A thick fog of steam coiled up into the sky, hissing and crackling, as the sea extinguished the fires raging in the lower decks. The Oginski twins' fortress upended and slipped into the waves, leaving a slick of oil and debris.

'Georgia!' Dakkar yelled.

He knew that nothing could survive the crash – and where was the *Nautilus*?

'What're you yelling about?' a voice above him asked.

A shadow blotted out the sun. Dakkar twisted his head around to see the familiar shape of the *Nautilus*, her balloons inflated.

'Georgia, thank goodness!' Dakkar just had time to say, then he hit the water hard.

The sea filled his ears and nostrils as he sank into the freezing depths. For a moment he wasn't sure which way was up and which was down. Bubbles surged around him and he kicked his way to the top, ignoring the stabbing pain in his legs and arms. The cold gnawed into his body, stealing his breath and making his teeth chatter almost instantly. He could barely kick his legs and the weight of the heavy furs he wore dragged him below the surface.

The *Nautilus* bellyflopped into the water with an undignified splash. The balloons hadn't had a chance to inflate fully and had only served to slow the craft's rapid descent.

Dakkar felt a numbness creeping over him. He felt so tired after all his adventures. It really would be pleasant to close his eyes and sleep …

Something splashed close to his face but he wasn't sure what it was.

'Dakkar!' Georgia called.

But Dakkar decided to ignore her and roll over. Whatever it was, it would keep until the morning. All he needed to do now was sleep.

Then something pulled at the hood of his jacket and Dakkar let himself be dragged through the water. Georgia looked down at him. She had a bargepole in her hands. She threw it aside and reached down, pulling him up.

Dakkar reached up but his arms felt like wet string and flopped back into the cold water with a splash. Then darkness took him.

*

Something flicked Dakkar's cheek hard. He groaned and turned over, relishing the delicious warmth that enveloped him. After weeks of skin-biting cold, it felt glorious to be bathed in heat, not having to worry about wearing gloves or furs or extra layers. But something flicked his face again. Dakkar waved his fingers across his face and winced. He ached – and that meant he was still alive. He opened one eye.

Georgia loomed over him, her red hair catching the glow of the Voltalith and the furnace that seemed to hum in unison inside the *Nautilus*'s engine room.

'What am I doing here?' Dakkar croaked, wincing as he tried to sit up. He looked down at the makeshift bed and the pile of damp furs that lay a few feet away.

'This was the warmest place to bring you,' Georgia said, smiling, but Dakkar could see the strain on her face. 'You were freezing when we pulled you out of the water. I didn't think you'd ever warm up again.'

'How long have I been asleep?' Dakkar said. His throat felt like sandpaper.

'Asleep?' Georgia said. 'Unconscious more than asleep. Nothing could rouse you. You've been out more than a day. We're heading back to Guthaven. Blizzard needs to know what's happened.'

Dakkar swallowed. 'How are we going to tell him that all his men are dead?'

Georgia just passed him a bottle of water. 'This is a bit stale but it's all we have,' she said.

It tasted like nectar to Dakkar and he had to be careful

not to drink it all. She handed him some dried meat which he chewed on gratefully.

'Tomasz fell,' Dakkar said at last. 'It wasn't … I didn't feel any … victory.'

Georgia gave a brief smile, her face sad. 'No,' she said. 'I know.'

Fletcher appeared with a fresh set of clothes – breeches, a shirt and a thick woollen jumper. He gave Dakkar a grin.

'Good to see you up and about, Dax,' he said, throwing the clothes at Dakkar. 'I reckon we've got a couple of days before we get to Guthaven so we should have your furs dried out by then if we keep them down here by the stove.'

Dakkar grinned back. 'Thanks. It's good to be warm again. I don't think I'll ever leave this room!'

'I'd better go and steer the *Nautilus*,' Georgia said, her cheeks reddening as Dakkar stretched out of the pile of blankets to reach the clothes. 'It would be a shame to crash and sink after all we've been through.'

She jumped up and bustled out of the engine room while Dakkar and Fletcher grinned at each other.

'Thanks for saving me,' Dakkar said quietly. 'I misjudged you when we first met. I'm sorry.'

'That's all right, Dax,' Fletcher said, getting up and heading for the door. 'You didn't leave me for dead, did you?'

'No, we didn't,' Dakkar admitted. 'And, Fletcher?'

'Yeah?' Fletcher said, turning back.

'It's Dakkar,' he said.

Fletcher laughed. 'All right, Dax.' He grinned and hurried out.

CHAPTER THIRTY-TWO
A GRATEFUL REUNION

HMS *Slaughter* looked a little less sorry for herself than when Dakkar had left. She no longer listed in the water and the main mast had been repaired.

'We've made good progress in the time you've been gone,' Blizzard said as he stood on the main deck with Dakkar, Georgia and Fletcher.

'I'm sorry we lost so many of your men,' Dakkar said. His heart felt heavy. 'We didn't stand a chance. The Tizheruk ...'

Blizzard raised his good hand. 'It's not your fault, Dakkar,' he said. 'You can't take responsibility for every man who falls in the line of duty. Tomàsz Oginski was to blame for those deaths, nobody else.'

'I know but ...'

'You still feel responsible,' Blizzard said. 'I know. So do I. It's the burden of leadership, something you'll have to become more accustomed to as time goes on. Besides, someone did make it back.'

'Baines?' Georgia said, turning round as three men strode gingerly up the gangplank.

'Morning, miss,' Sergeant Baines said, saluting. 'Oh, now then, miss,' he added as Georgia wrapped her arms around his burly chest. 'Salter and Atwood made it too.'

The two marines behind Baines grinned at his discomfort.

'Put 'im down, Miss Georgia – you don't know where he's been,' Fletcher said, grinning.

'Good to see you haven't lost your sense of humour, lad,' Baines said, giving Fletcher a hearty slap on the back that nearly sent the boy tumbling to the deck.

'I'm glad you made it back, sergeant,' Dakkar said, shaking his hand. 'I thought you were lost for ever in that storm.'

'So did we, sir,' Baines said. 'But Salter here, he dug us a hole and we sat the storm out. I thought he'd gone mad but he said he'd seen one of them Inuits do it once many years ago when he was shipwrecked on a whaling vessel round these parts.'

'We searched for you, sir,' said Atwood, a thin dark-haired man. 'But the storm wiped out any footprints and we barely had enough supplies to get us back.'

'We all did our level best, Atwood,' Blizzard said steadily. 'The Heart of Vulcan has been destroyed and two more of the Oginski brothers are no longer a threat to our nation's common good.'

'Three Oginski brothers died, commander,' Dakkar said quietly.

'Quite. I hadn't forgotten,' Blizzard said. 'Oginski was a hero. He died saving your life.'

'He was part of a cruel trick played by Borys,' Dakkar murmured. 'His own brother. I'm sick of revenge and I'm sick of the Oginskis' family feud.'

'The threat remains, however,' Blizzard said. 'I've a horrible feeling that the remaining Brothers Oginski will come looking for you whether you're sick of them or not.'

'I know, commander,' Dakkar said. 'I'm sure they will.'

'Then you will continue to pursue Cryptos?' Blizzard said, eyebrows raised.

'No. I'll not go looking for them,' Dakkar said. 'But if they come looking for me, I'll be ready.'

'And you have our full support,' Blizzard said. He paused and looked at Dakkar closely. 'You will join us now, I assume? We can offer you support and shelter – and the utmost secrecy. Join Project Nemo.'

Dakkar looked hard at Blizzard. Project Nemo was Blizzard's secret army and navy, elite soldiers dedicated to defeating a common enemy, the Brothers Oginski and the organisation they called Cryptos. He cast his gaze across Georgia and Fletcher.

'It seems I already have a crew for my submersible, commander,' he said. 'But, yes, we will join you. From now on, the *Nautilus* sails for Project Nemo.'

'The baton of responsibility has been passed, Dakkar,' Blizzard said, shaking his hand. 'Count Oginski would be proud of you.'

A NOTE FROM THE AUTHOR

THE *NAUTILUS* FLIES!

Given that Prince Dakkar is the young Captain Nemo, Jules Verne's tortured hero from *Twenty Thousand Leagues Under the Sea* and *The Mysterious Island*, I wanted to bring Verne's fascination with flight into the third *Monster Odyssey* book. Verne wrote a number of books based on hot-air balloons and flying machines – *Around the World in Eighty Days* is probably the most famous of these stories. But he also wrote *The Master of the World*, about an amphibious flying machine that can travel at incredible speed. With these stories in mind, I wanted to take the *Nautilus* into the clouds!

VOLTALITHS AND THERMOLITHS

As far as I know, electrically charged meteors don't actually exist, nor do meteors that generate heat spontaneously. But Verne did write a book called *The Chase of the Golden Meteor*, which tells the story of two astronomers competing to retrieve a valuable meteorite.

LANDS OF ICE AND SNOW

As someone who wrote about amazing journeys, Jules Verne included expeditions to the North and South Poles in many of his stories. The quotation at the beginning of this book is from *The Adventures of Captain Hatteras*, which was published in 1864. This tells of an Englishman's mission to travel to the North Pole and his adventures there. In *Twenty Thousand Leagues Under the Sea*, Captain Nemo discovers the South Pole. As a young boy, I loved watching the Disney films *The Land That Time Forgot* and *The People That Time Forgot*. These were based on novels by Edgar Rice Burroughs and are set in prehistoric worlds hidden in the North and South Poles. Another favourite of mine was the Marvel Comics character Ka-Zar, a Tarzan type who lives under Antarctica in the Savage Lands. Ka-Zar fights dinosaurs and other prehistoric threats. When I was thinking of a setting for this book, the polar wastes sprang to mind.

MONSTERS

The Tizheruk is taken from Inuit folklore – the Inuit do a great line in creatures that can slither out of the frozen waters and drag you in. Hideous little monsters that pull to their doom those foolish enough to wander near deep water can be found in most cultures. The Qalupalik are a variation on water sprites, Jenny Greenteeth and the nixie. The sharks in the ice cave's pool are Greenland sharks. There is much controversy about this shark's feeding habits and whether it is a predator or a scavenger but I decided to make it big and nasty.

HISTORICAL EVENTS

In the latter half of 1815, most of Europe was still reacting to the downfall of Emperor Napoléon Bonaparte at the Battle of Waterloo. Mount Tambora, on an island in present-day Indonesia, did erupt in this year. Huge quantities of volcanic ash were thrown up into the atmosphere, affecting the weather and causing 1816 to be called 'the year with no summer'.

Look out for more
Monster Odyssey adventures

Also available in this series: *Monster Odyssey: The Eye of Neptune*

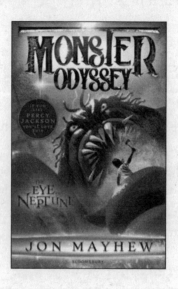

Prince Dakkar, heir to an Indian kingdom, has been expelled from the best schools in England. Now he's stuck with the mysterious Count Oginski, genius inventor of a top-secret machine: the world's first submersible.

But in a dangerous world of spies and secrecy, someone would do anything to capture Oginski's invention. When the count is kidnapped, Dakkar escapes in the submarine, only to face horrifying creatures of the deep, lethal giant squid, and, above all, the sinister Cryptos, who is hell-bent on taking over the world . . .

Also available in this series: *Monster Odyssey: The Wrath of the Lizard Lord*

When a dangerous mission goes wrong, Dakkar and Oginski
are attacked by a hideous lizard-like creature. Oginski is
badly wounded in the attack, leaving Dakkar to search
for clues to the origins of the monster lizard alone.

His search leads him to an ancient world hidden deep below
the surface of the earth, where he discovers a terrifying army
poised for battle above ground – but trapped beneath
the earth himself, how can Dakkar stop them?

And don't miss . . .

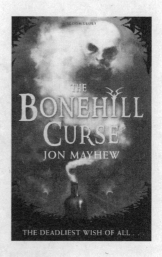